FALL GUY
– who *really* killed his wife?

The third book in the Detective Chief Inspector Harvey
Livermore series

Tony Flood

best wishes
Tony Flood

FALL GUY
– who *really* killed his wife?

Published in the UK in December, 2022 by
Tony Flood in conjunction with
SW Communications.

PRAISE FOR
FALL GUY
– who *really* killed his wife?

Tony Flood keeps us guessing until a stunning final twist. Excellent characters in a gripping, fast-paced, authentic whodunit. **- GRAHAM BARTLETT, former police Chief Superintendent and author of crime thriller Bad for Good.**

Talented former journalist Tony Flood made an exciting entry into the world of crime writing by treating thriller fans to a 'Triple Tease'. Tony's shrewd copper DCI Harvey Livermore continues to unravel baffling murder cases. **- PETER JAMES, international best-selling thriller writer.**

A fast-paced thriller that will keep you turning the pages right up to the final, shocking twist. Packed full of sharp dialogue and memorable characters, this is a great read **- SHEILA BUGLER, author of the acclaimed Dee Doran crime series.**

Tony Flood has created one of the best modern day fictional cops in Harvey Livermore. The astute DCI listens to others and acts decisively - as he does when a distraught Myra Thornhill insists new evidence suggests her brother George was wrongly convicted for the murder of his wife.

A captivating read by one of my favourite authors
- **JEANNETTE HENSBY, True Crime Writer.**

In Tony Flood's cleverly constructed thriller, we are told at the start that George Thornhill did not kill his wife, but all the evidence shows he did. So he is convicted and relies on his sister Myra to persuade DCI Livermore to reopen the case.

New suspects emerge in a spine-tingling tale populated by police characters from Tony's previous two crime thrillers.

This ingenious story keeps us on the edge of our seats throughout as the tension increases. Join George's shattering ride while his sister tries to convince everyone of his innocence. - **JOHN NEWTON, author, broadcaster and former police officer.**

Fall Guy is an ideal crime thriller for fans of Peter James, James Patterson and Michael Connelly. Excellent plot and characters, with touches of humour relieving the tension. - **FRANCIS WAIT, author of Android Affair.**

CREDITS:

FRONT COVER PICTURE IMAGE BY:
alphaspirit (depositphotos)

BACK COVER PICTURE IMAGE BY:
kantver (depositphotos)

COVERS DESIGNED by:
Emmy Ellis https://studioenp.com/

BOOK CONTENTS FORMATTED by:
James Harvey – Badgoose Publishing
https://soulsong.co.uk

YOU QUALIFY FOR
A FREE BOOK

As a 'thank you' for buying FALL GUY, author Tony Flood is offering you one of his other books FREE.

To obtain a complimentary e-version just choose one of the books shown at the end of this novel and email your choice to Tony at tflood04@yahoo.co.uk He will email you back with the e-version as an attachment.

The author also makes donations to Children with Cancer UK from his paperback sales. You can help by writing a review if you enjoy them.

ACKNOWLEDGEMENTS

I owe a huge debt of gratitude to GRAHAM BARTLETT, former police Chief Superintendent and author of crime thriller Bad for Good, for his extremely helpful advice on police procedures. By answering my stream of questions and making helpful suggestions, Graham has ensured that Fall Guy has credibility and authenticity.

I'm also very grateful to Graham and fellow authors PETER JAMES, SHEILA BUGLER, JOHN NEWTON, FRANCIS WAIT and JEANNETTE HENSBY for providing excellent endorsements for Fall Guy, myself and my DCI Harvey Livermore.

More big 'thank yous' are due to my wife and fellow author HEATHER FLOOD, TAMARA MCKINLEY, who writes international best-sellers under Ellie Dean, and JOHN NEWTON for giving me further feedback, ideas and encouragement during the seemingly never-ending re-writing and editing process.

Many thanks also to JAMES HARVEY of Badgoose Publishing and EMMY ELLIS of Studioenp for their first-class formatting and cover designs respectively as well as giving valuable advice.

FALL GUY

PART ONE

CHAPTER ONE

Wednesday October 6th, 2021

George Thornhill interrupted a business meeting with a client to accept a phone call from his gorgeous wife Isabella on her 32nd birthday. She simply said: "I'm wearing the black kimono you gave me this morning - and nothing else!"

"Nothing? What if someone comes round?"

"You'd better get home before they do, darling," she teased, and then rang off.

George, the owner of a construction company in Lewes, apologised to the client, and agreed a much more generous deal than he had intended so he could wrap things up early.

He rushed to his Nissan Qashqai to avoid getting drenched by the rain, and, before driving off, checked that the clock on the dashboard corresponded with his watch. He smiled at seeing they both showed 2.07pm - five minutes fast, as he always set them, to help him avoid his tendency of being late.

'Blimey! I'm actually ahead of schedule for once, and I'll miss the mid-afternoon Friday traffic in Eastbourne - Isabella will be surprised. There'll be time for some birthday nooky before we go out to dinner this evening.'

George's thoughts focused on his wife's hourglass figure which had made her so successful as a fashion model.

The sharp blast of a car horn ended his daydream abruptly. He suddenly realised his Nissan was drifting dangerously towards the opposite traffic lane and quickly adjusted the steering wheel. The car skidded on the wet surface, but corrected itself when he turned into the skid.

George chastised himself for his lapse into a flight of fantasy almost causing an accident.

'It could be due to the Sumatriptan I've started taking for my migraines,' he thought. 'They might be causing me to feel dizzy and my mind to wander. I'd better check with the doctor.'

He sped past a 30mph sign before he regained his concentration. 'Damn, I'm doing almost 40. I should have taken the alternative route, then I wouldn't be risking getting caught again by this bloody speed trap.' He slowed to 25mph, determined not to incur another motoring fine to add to the one he had received a few months back.

Even so, George had time to stop off to buy a large bouquet of flowers and still park in the drive of his stylish, semi-detached bungalow in Langney at three o'clock - 3.05pm by his watch!

He looked in the car mirror to check his mass of

brown hair was as well groomed as possible. 'Not bad', he thought, stroking his chin where the only blemish was a small scar caused by a fall many years ago. George picked up the flowers from the passenger seat, opened the nearside door and slid out.

After nodding to an elderly neighbour who was hurrying to avoid the rain by getting into his old Honda, George opened his front door, calling out "Hello, darling."

Startled by a sound of groaning from the lounge, he dropped the flowers and hurried into the room to be met with the terrible sight of Isabella lying on the floor with a knife in her chest. Blood was gushing from a large wound, soaking her black satin kimono and the carpet.

"Isabella!" he yelled. "Oh, my God, what's happened?"

George rushed to his wife's side and heard her gasp something inaudible.

His first instinct was to pull out the knife, but was aware that it could make such injuries even worse.

He tried pressing down on either side of the wound and pushing the opening together. His efforts were in vain and blood continued to flow.

'What else can I do?' he thought. 'It might help to take the damn thing out.' He grabbed the handle, removed the kitchen knife from the wound and threw it on the floor before trying again to seal the large gash.

But Isabella's eyes, pale blue like his own, slowly closed and she stopped breathing.

George gave mouth-to-mouth resuscitation without getting any response. He felt his wife's wrist for a pulse - there was none.

In desperation he shook the motionless body, causing flecks of blood to spread to her long blonde hair and his own, before finally accepting he could not bring her back to life.

"No, no, no," the distraught husband cried out, sobbing uncontrollably and holding her close to him.

When George fully grasped the situation, he telephoned the police.

In the 14 minutes before they arrived he protected his dead wife's 'modesty' by pulling together the kimono he had given her as a birthday present that morning so that her breasts were no longer exposed.

+++++

George, whose blue suit and hands were still covered in blood, told the lead officer DI Jeff

Nottage how he'd tried desperately to save his wife without success.

But he found it hard to concentrate on what the policeman was saying in response. His grief, coupled with the effects of the Sumatriptan he took, was causing a feeling of nausea to sweep over him.

'I'd better breathe in and out slowly or I'm going to throw up,' George thought. If he needed a distraction it was provided by the Scene of Crime Officers, dressed in protective clothing, scrutinizing everything in sight.

The whole thing seemed a blur, including being driven to Eastbourne Custody Suite where his blood-covered suit and other clothing were taken for examination. The nausea was replaced by numbness as he sat in a sweatshirt, jogging bottoms and plimsolls provided by the police, but he tried to collect his thoughts upon being further questioned by Nottage and another officer.

George became aware that their tone had changed from that when he first encountered them. "I'm not feeling up to answering any more questions at the moment," he said. "Is it alright if I go now?"

He was shocked when Nottage replied: "You don't seem to realise the full implications of what I told you earlier, sir."

"My wife's death has been devastating. I wasn't fully focused on what you were saying. Remind me."

Nottage spelt it out. "I referred to you being covered in blood and, by your own admission, you held the knife that killed your wife. There was no trace of anyone else having been present so I had no alternative but to tell you that I was arresting you on suspicion of murder. I should remind you that you do not have to say anything unless you wish to do so. But it may harm your defence if you do not mention when questioned something which you later rely on in court. Anything you do say may be given in evidence."

CHAPTER TWO
Thursday, October 7th, 2021

DI Nottage was worried at being put in charge of a murder case within days of his long-standing boss, DCI Harvey Livermore, going off sick to be treated for lung cancer.

'Don't be so stupid', he rebuked himself. 'You're fully up to the task, and this case couldn't be more straight forward. Getting a conviction will look good on your CV.'

He was waiting for a forensics report but was certain it would confirm that the blood in which George Thornhill had been covered was that of his wife, and the prints on the lethal weapon, a kitchen knife found on the floor about two metres from the body, were those of himself.

Nottage, a normally likeable, open-minded officer, adopted his most uncompromising face as he relayed these findings to George and his solicitor David Palmer while conducting questioning with the assistance of DS Chris Dimbleby in the small, windowless interview room at Eastbourne.

"The facts speak for themselves," the bespectacled DI said gravely, looking up from his notes.

Palmer responded: "We don't dispute the findings, but you've come to the wrong conclusion, Inspector. My client has told you repeatedly that he removed the knife from his wife's wound in a last desperate attempt to save her because he could not stem the blood flowing from it. Someone else had already committed the crime. My client has been consistent in both what he said at the scene of the crime and in his statement."

"That's right," added George. "Why won't you accept that I returned home to find my wife lying wounded on the floor? I simply went to her aid."

The DI maintained a dour expression and shook his head. But before he could speak DS Mike O'Sullivan entered the room. Nottage announced this for the benefit of the tape recording, and upon reading a written message that O'Sullivan had brought him, suppressed a smile. He then restarted the interview when his colleague had departed.

"You claim that you came home to discover your wife had been attacked, Mr Thornhill. But the more obvious explanation is that you stabbed her yourself. The fact your wife's prints are also on blood on the knife, partly covered by those of your own, suggests she may have used it to defend herself. The obvious conclusion is that you snatched it from her and caused the injuries."

"That's not what happened," protested George. "You should be searching for who did this terrible crime - not falsely accusing me of it. Perhaps it was a robbery that went wrong."

"The evidence does not support what you're suggesting," Nottage replied. "There were no signs of a break-in."

A perspiring George persisted. "Then perhaps it was someone Isabella knew and she let them in."

Nottage was about to answer but was side-tracked by Palmer. The solicitor, having crossed one leg over the other to knock a speck of dirt off his expensive Dolce & Gabbana designer shoes with gold chains, asked: "Was anyone else seen entering the bungalow before George got home?"

'Flash sod', thought an irritated Nottage. 'Perhaps I'm in the wrong job. I'm having to make do with glasses from Specsavers and a cheap watch while solicitors like this are decked out in designer watches, cuff links and shoes'.

His hesitation resulted in Palmer asking again: "Was anyone seen entering, Inspector?"

"No," replied Nottage, shaking his head firmly and readjusting his glasses.

"Well, was anyone seen leaving?" queried Palmer.

Nottage felt he needed to regain the initiative and it gave him great satisfaction to put the legal practitioner in his place. "The neighbours have been questioned and none of them can remember seeing anyone entering or leaving before Mr Thornhill parked in the drive. Furthermore, I've just been informed by my colleague that Express Couriers delivered a parcel half an hour before Mr Thornhill said he arrived at three o'clock - allowing for his watch being five minutes fast! That proves Mrs Thornhill was very much alive half an hour prior to his arrival because she signed for the parcel at 2.29pm."

Following a brief silence, Nottage continued: "This leaves a very narrow time frame in which someone else could have killed her and somehow departed unseen. The most salient fact is that your client has admitted his wife died after his arrival."

He gave the briefest of nods to his long serving colleague Dimbleby who spoke for the first time. "We have no other suspects. And in all my years in the force this is the most open-and-shut case I've ever come across."

+++++

Jeff Nottage repeated Dimbleby's words when reporting to Detective Chief Superintendent 'Fussy' Frampton.

"Yes," replied the fastidious Frampton, "it certainly seems to be an open-and-shut case on the face of it, despite the husband's insistence he didn't do it. Do you think there's any possibility at all that he could be telling the truth?"

"No sir. It's simply not realistic for someone else to have arrived after Mrs Thornhill took a delivery, killed her and then departed in the half hour before her husband got home. The bungalows in the street are all within clear sight of each other and none of the neighbours, nor the delivery man, saw anyone enter or leave No. 24, The Haven. Even Mr Thornhill himself says he did not see or hear anyone."

"I agree with you, Jeff."

Nottage felt relieved that his senior officer, known throughout the Sussex force for his insistence on ticking every box before making a decision, was concurring.

However, Frampton's intake and slow release of breath suggested there might be a proviso. And it quickly followed. "I think we should go to the CPS for authority to charge, Jeff. But if Thornhill changes his story and admits to stabbing his wife unintentionally then the CPS may change the charge to manslaughter. And I would have to support that."

Nottage frowned as his boss continued: "Thornhill could say his wife was the one who first grabbed hold of the knife which I understand she had left in the lounge, apparently to cut open the wrappings of some of her birthday presents. His defence would presumably be that he did not mean to kill her."

This caused Nottage to protest. "But the knife thrust must have been made with force for it to penetrate so far."

Frampton met his younger officer's gaze as he answered: "Thornhill's barrister can claim that the blade went deeper when the body hit the floor."

He picked up a report from his desk and read from it. "The medical findings say a single stab wound entered the front of the left side of the chest between the second and third ribs to a depth of 12cm. It penetrated the two chambers of the right side of the heart, causing damage to the ventricular wall and bleeding into the lungs. This wound, and the bleeding that resulted from it, was the cause of death."

Frampton looked up before giving a summary. "It's unlikely that Thornhill intended to inflict such serious injuries."

Nottage was unconvinced. "His assertion that he didn't do it should be his downfall, sir. When the forensic evidence is complete it could prove conclusively that he's lying. I think we'll get a murder verdict."

"You may well be right, Jeff. Rest assured that Thornhill won't get let off lightly - he's facing a stiff sentence. And there's no question of him being given bail during the lengthy time it will take for this case to get to court."

Tony Flood

CHAPTER THREE

October, 2021 to February, 2022

Myra Thornhill, a community worker who helped people with physical disabilities and mental health needs, fully appreciated how her brother was suffering from deep depression during the months spent on remand in Lewes Prison.

She made an appointment to discuss the problem with his solicitor David Parsons, about whom she had mixed feelings.

Myra, unmarried and in her early thirties, respected Parsons for his vast knowledge of the law and for being her brother's long-standing friend, but found him rather pompous and self indulgent. His silk tie, initialled cuff links, Rolex watch and even more expensive shoes confirmed her opinion.

"Look, David, I'm worried sick about George. Being stuck in Lewes Prison all this time is affecting his mental health. Is there nothing we can do?"

In a tone full of sympathy. Parsons said: "It's dreadful what George is going through, but unfortunately it may be months before he's given a trial date."

Myra, normally so strong and unshakeable, felt tears welling in her eyes. "It's just such an awful situation - not only for George but for our mother, too. She suffers from kidney disease and the worry of all this is making her health worse. Unfortunately, she's not well enough to visit him. As far as I know, only you and I go to see him."

"I'll continue to do so," Parsons assured her. "We've been friends since we were in the university cricket team. He's a great bloke and I know there's no way he would have it in him to kill Isabella."

Myra wiped the tears from her pale, drawn Elfin-like face, and looked in a new light at the man she had up to now considered to be 'a stuck-up prat'.

"Thank you, David. We greatly appreciate your support during this terrible time. What makes things worse is that there are still hostile stories appearing about George in the Press. Some of the papers have made silly references to George and Isabella as 'beauty and the beast' and even the pictures they've used have helped to portray that image. Photos taken of Isabella while modelling, showing a glamorous, fresh-faced beauty, are in complete contrast with an over-used unflattering snatched shot of George."

She received a nod of acknowledgement from Parsons, but then noticed the self-centred man glance at his Rolex watch.

Trying to refrain from thinking of him as a prat again, she said: "George doesn't know what the Press have been saying, but he's distraught that Isabella's parents, together with most of his friends and contacts, have cut themselves off from him. They ignored him at the funeral. These people don't realise that, far from being her killer, he's heart-broken to have lost the woman he loved. He's not been given any opportunity to grieve properly, and the deep depression he's experiencing is having a very harmful effect on him."

Parsons promised: "I'll speak to George's barrister to see if there's anything that can be done to speed things up."

The result was that the prosecution agreed to an earlier trial date as a courtroom became available at the Old Bailey.

Tony Flood

CHAPTER FOUR

Wednesday, April 13th to Friday, May 27th, 2022

George, although relieved to finally get a chance to defend himself, found it intimidating appearing at the Old Bailey, the most famous criminal court in the world.

Standing outside looking up at the famous Statue of Justice, a powerful woman holding scales in one hand and an upright sword in the other, was bad enough, but being in the dock listening to the charge of murder read out proved even worse.

He also felt deeply embarrassed that some of his relatives and friends - now ex-friends - were watching from the public gallery. Only his sister Myra and his elderly mother seemed to be showing concern - the others, he felt, were there to see him get his comeuppance.

But the most daunting experience was having to endure listening to the police and forensic evidence which showed the relevant fingerprints, footprints, hairs and fibres were his.

George cringed as Nottage told the court: "Mr Thornhill's claim that someone else committed this crime does not equate with the facts that have come to light. Not only was he covered in his wife's blood, but his fingerprints were on the knife and his DNA on her mouth, her wrist and kimono."

Defence counsel Jason Smallbone tried to dismiss this seemingly damning evidence. He strenuously cross-examined Nottage, claiming it could all be explained by George removing the knife and his attempts at both mouth-to-mouth resuscitation and chest compressions as well as taking his wife's pulse before covering her nakedness by closing her kimono.

But the policeman's only small concession was to say "While Mr Thornhill's version of events is possible, it is so highly improbable that I find it to be unbelievable. Removing the knife from the wound would go against all medical advice, and taking her pulse would not account for there being a bruise on Mrs Thornhill's wrist."

'You bastard,' thought George. 'You've been rehearsing that little speech, haven't you?'

As the trial progressed things did not get any better, and George felt the evidence of the Express Couriers driver, an Irishman with receding hair called Donal McCarthy, to be almost as damaging.

McCarthy recounted how Isabella had appeared to be "calm and cheerful" when signing for a parcel at 2.29pm - 31 minutes prior to George's arrival.

He was sure of the time because "I went off duty at two-thirty."

George became aware that McCarthy had an occasional eye twitch, and prayed that the little Irishman would falter. But the driver never wavered under cross-examination and insisted he had neither seen nor heard anyone at The Haven apart from Isabella.

Jason Smallbone challenged him. "Is it possible that someone was in her lounge, out of your sight and hearing?"

"That's possible but unlikely, sir. And there were no vehicles parked outside - I remember that part of the road being clear."

An elderly grey-haired neighbour then told the court that he had seen George arrive home at 3pm.

"How can you be certain of the time?" asked Smallbone, peering over his spectacles.

The old man answered without hesitation. "I was getting into my car and driving to pick up my wife. I was due to collect her from the doctor's nearby at 3.15pm. George drove into his drive at the same time as I was leaving."

George cursed his luck that the prosecution witnesses seemed so positive.

He felt less assured when giving his own evidence, but repeated what he had said in his statement. "I came home and found my wife had been stabbed. I did everything I could think of to save her. It was to no use and, despite trying to stem the bleeding from her wound and give mouth-to-mouth resuscitation, she died within minutes."

George broke down, sobbing, under cross-examination. The Prosecution counsel Peter Urquhart showed no sympathy and said: "I put it to you that you had an argument with your wife and attacked her."

"That's complete nonsense!"

Urquhart was insistent: "The facts suggest otherwise."

"There are no facts!" bellowed George, for which he was rebuked by Judge Nathan Hopkins, an Old Etonian with a clipped accent.

"Sorry, My Lord. But my wife and I loved each other and were about to celebrate her birthday. We had nothing to argue about. She had phoned me to tell me she was wearing the kimono I had given her and suggested I came home early. She was inviting me to have sex with her."

Urquhart was quick to pounce on this interpretation. "You were obviously under a misapprehension, Mr Thornhill. It was when your wife refused to have sex that you attacked her, wasn't it?"

"No! You've got it completely wrong. Someone else stabbed her."

This assertion was mocked by Urquhart. "Ah, yes. This mysterious someone who nobody saw enter or leave - not even you. Your story has so many flaws in it, including your claim that you thought it would help by pulling the knife from the wound."

"I couldn't stop the bleeding," George retorted. "I'd tried doing so while the knife was in the wound and thought it might help to take it out."

He could sense his evidence was being treated with scepticism. George's concerns continued when most of the jurors refused to make eye contact with him as they left the courtroom to reach their verdict and as they returned around four hours later.

'It's a bad sign', thought the fretful defendant.

He was proved right. The foreman, a middle-aged man with a bulbous nose, announced in a gruff voice: "Guilty."

Judge Hopkins told the broken man in front of him: "I have listened carefully to the pleas given on your behalf by your sister and your solicitor, pointing out that you are a man of previous good character with no convictions. But, far from showing any remorse, you have persisted in claiming you did not carry out the fateful attack on your wife. There is damning evidence to the contrary that shows you're lying."

He paused and added: "I am sentencing you to life imprisonment, with a minimum term of 15 years less the time already served on remand..."

George didn't hear the rest of the judge's words. He almost collapsed with shock and had to be helped from the dock.

FALL GUY

PART TWO

CHAPTER FIVE

Friday, May 27th to
Thursday, June 9th, 2022

George Thornhill's first two weeks in Her Majesty's category A prison Belmarsh were more traumatic than his time on remand in Lewes.

The entrance, with its foreboding high walls and electric gates, made George fearful of what lay ahead. But nothing prepared him for a confrontation in the food hall at lunch time on day four. George was deep in thought about his predicament and not paying attention as he walked towards the seating area with his tray of food.

He bumped into a fellow inmate, knocking the other man's tray of food out of his hand and causing it to clatter on the floor.

George, a well built 17-stone, 35-year-old, was hardly short at six foot two inches, but his adversary towered over him as he shouted: "You stupid bastard!"

A stammered "sorry" did not stop the irate giant lifting him off his feet with one hand and giving him a slap on the face with the other. "If you ever do anything like that again you'll be in a hospital bed."

"It was an accident," George muttered as he was

released and fell to the floor. "You're quite welcome to take my tray."

"Bloody right I will. We'll do a swap, with you picking up every scrap of what I've dropped and eating it."

George felt completely humiliated having to scrape the food off the dirty floor and stuff it into his mouth while his fellow diners derided him.

The thug strode over as he picked up the last morsel and trod on his hand, causing him to yelp in pain. Only then did a guard intervene.

It did not give George any comfort when he was told later by his cell-mate Fats Brown "You got off lightly!"

"You think so, do you?"

"Yeah. The bloke you bumped into was Mad Micky Moore. He's a vicious sod who's serving life for chopping up a thug from a rival gang. I'd keep out of Micky's way if I was you."

George heeded the advice. But he was finding the whole experience in Belmarsh awful - from the uncomfortable mattress on his cramped bed in a cell eight foot by twelve foot to the constant noise of other inmates banging, shouting and arguing.

His migraines were becoming more frequent and his depression increasingly worse.

CHAPTER SIX

Thursday, June 9th, 2022

George tried to put on a brave face when his sister Myra came to visit him in Belmarsh.

"Hello, Elfin," he greeted, using the nick-name he'd given her since their teens because of Myra's closely cropped hair which complimented her short, upturned nose and eyes, and patulous lips.

But George's bonhomie did not last long as they sat facing each other at one of the many tables in the visitors hall.

"I'm going mad in here, Elfin," he blurted out between gritted teeth. "If I could I'd top myself."

"Don't allow yourself to think like that, George," Myra pleaded, her pale features twisting into a grimace. "There's always hope - never give up."

He forced a faint smile and became aware that his sister had spotted the swelling on his face.

"What's that mark, George?" Have the prison officers hurt you?"

"No, it was just a slight 'misunderstanding' with a fellow inmate I accidentally bumped into and he showed his displeasure. It's all sorted out now."

"You should make a complaint to the Governor."

"No, that would result in a lot more trouble. It's best forgotten about, Elfin."

She reached out her hand to him across the table at which they were seated opposite each other in the visiting hall, but pulled it back when a prison officer shot her a warning look.

"Sorry, Myra. But being stuck in a tiny cell and mixing with some of the country's most vicious thugs every day is hard to take. There's no privacy, the noise is unbearable and everything stinks of sweat and piss - including my cellmate."

He clenched his fists as he spoke. "My life has literally changed from heaven to hell. Isabella and I had a wonderful life after moving into our dream home - we even called it 'Haven' because it was so lovely and peaceful, away from the stresses of the outside world. This bloody prison is the exact opposite."

His sister nodded sympathetically and pushed away a strand of her blonde hair that had fallen over her forehead.

"I've spoken to your solicitor David Palmer and he says we would need to come up with some new evidence in order to make an appeal. So I'm going to try to find some."

"What do you mean?"

"I'm going to talk to your neighbours. One of them might have seen whoever killed Isabella either arrive or leave. The police say they spoke to them but maybe they need their memories jogging. I can do that."

"That's very good of you, Elfin, but it's a remote chance, isn't it? I can't understand why nobody saw anything. Even the Express Couriers guy said there was no car in our drive or outside."

Myra agreed. "Perhaps whoever attacked Isabella parked further down the street. And they may have already been inside your bungalow at the time she went to the front door to receive the delivery."

"So why didn't Isabella ask the delivery man to help her."

"It could have been someone she knew. They might not have seemed a threat to her at first. Maybe the situation changed after the delivery man had gone."

George ran his hand over the stubble on his chin, pondering this scenario. "That would make sense. But it's impossible to prove, isn't it?"

Tony Flood

CHAPTER SEVEN

Tuesday, June 14th, 2022

DCI Harvey Livermore's decision to delay an operation so that he could solve a previous case had almost proved fatal.

The surgeon, who removed a cancerous lobe from his right lung, told him: "If you'd left it any longer you might not be with us now."

Livermore found the recovery period harder to endure than the operation itself, especially as his wife Evelyne was even more inclined to nit-pick than his boss Fussy Frampton.

He was relieved to get back to work, though he found it frustrating being confined to office duties while Nottage prepared for the prosecution of George Thornhill and then gave evidence against him.

Three weeks after the verdict, Livermore was sitting in a cafe across the road from police HQ in Lewes, eating his lunch, when a woman in her thirties approached him.

"I believe you're in charge of the serious crimes team," she said.

"That's right," he replied. "Actually it's the Surrey and Sussex Major Crime Team."

"My name is Myra Thornhill. I'm the sister of George Thornhill."

"I'm sorry but I cannot discuss the case with you," Livermore told her. "I was not involved in the investigation."

"But you're the head man, aren't you," she insisted. "I just want to give you some vital information which may cause you to reopen it."

"You should make an appointment to see me. I'm trying to eat my lunch."

Myra ignored his suggestion and took a seat in the chair opposite him. "I don't think I'm asking much of you to spare me ten minutes of your time when my brother is in prison, feeling suicidal, after being given a fifteen-year sentence for a crime he did not commit."

The woman's impassioned plea, combined with signs of strain emphasised by a minimal use of make-up on her elfin-like face, won Livermore over.

"OK," he agreed, pushing the remainder of his salmon salad to one side. "What is this information?"

"I've been speaking to the neighbours in the bungalows next to where Isabella and George lived at No. 24. One of them, a young lady called Ruth Jenner, tells me she saw someone leave

George's home by the backdoor on the afternoon Isabella was killed."

Livermore's bushy eyebrows shot up as he expressed his surprise. "I find that hard to accept. The officers on the case interviewed all the neighbours and none of them saw anyone enter or leave the crime scene apart from George."

"Your officers messed up. Ruth lives with her parents two doors along from George, but she flew to France early the day after the attack. She'd left for a three-week camping holiday with some friends by the time police questioned her mother and father. They did not see anyone at George's home, but Ruth did. That surely proves someone else was with Isabella and was the person who stabbed her - not George."

"Alright, I'll look into it," Livermore assured her.

"You shouldn't find it hard to come up with suspects, Chief Inspector. There's an obvious one in that nut case Hayden Stubbs who Isabella had reported to the police for stalking her. You might also include Isabella's brother-in-law Brandon Cunningham."

"Why's that?"

"He's a womaniser and he had the hots for her. But he wasn't the only one. As a model, she got a lot of attention from men."

+++++

Myra left feeling that her meeting with Livermore had gone well.

The policeman had agreed to look into what she'd told him, and she believed he would do so.

Livermore's manner impressed her, as did the rugged look of the man, with his strong jaw, wide cheekbones and penetrating granite grey eyes. Myra could forgive him his lack of fashion sense, as demonstrated by a sports jacket last considered trendy ten years ago. The important thing was she felt she could trust him.

CHAPTER EIGHT
Tuesday, June 14th, 2022

Livermore called Nottage into his office and informed him of what Myra Thornhill was claiming.

"I've looked through the statements given by neighbours and there's nothing from this young lady Ruth Jenner who Myra Thornhill has spoken to. It seems that because she left for some foreign junket the day after the murder, we overlooked her."

"So what do you suggest, Guv?"

"Let's send Dimbleby and Conteh to interview Miss Jenner and see what she's got to say."

+++++

DC Grace Conteh felt the name Ruth Jenner was familiar but could not quite place it as she travelled with DS Dimbleby to interview the woman at her parents' home.

But Jenner's over-stated dress style and make-up, together with her uncooperative manner, helped Grace remember that she had crossed paths with her a few years previously. That was when Grace was a young PC on her first drugs bust.

Her thoughts were interrupted by the fiery red-head's unhelpful response to what Dimbleby was asking about the death of her neighbour. She replied defiantly: "Isabella was killed ages ago so why do you want to talk to me about it now? And how do you expect me to remember what happened back then?"

"You seemed to remember well enough when you spoke to George Thornhill's sister," Dimbleby countered.

"That was a private conversation," retorted the indignant young woman whose red hair had been dyed with streaks of blue. "I've nothing to say to you lot."

Conteh decided it was time to refer to her previous encounter with Jenner. "You don't like the police much, do you, Ruth? Could that have anything to do with the fact you were among the party-goers we arrested a couple of years ago in relation to peddling cannabis and cocaine?"

"Too right! You bastards should concentrate on running in real villains instead of hounding druggies."

Conteh tried to reason with her. "This isn't anything to do with what you think about the police - it's doing the right thing by your neighbours."

Jenner seemed to consider the point and finally relented.

"Alright, I'll tell you what I told George's sister. On the afternoon of the murder I saw someone leave George's bungalow through the back door. They used the gate at the bottom of the garden to go into the path at the rear of the bungalows."

"What sort of time would that have been?" asked Dimbleby.

Ruth seemed to go into a trace and did not answer.

Conteh studied the woman and could tell from her bloodshot eyes and slight involuntary shaking that she was still into drugs. The policewoman gently reminded her: "My colleague asked you what time of day that was?"

"I can't be certain, but it must have been about an hour before you lot arrived in all your police cars."

"Can you describe who you saw?" Dimbleby pressed.

"No. I only got a brief glimpse through our kitchen window while I was pouring myself a glass of water."

Conteh wanted to know more. "Were you looking through a lace curtain or did you have a clear view?"

"There's no curtain on our kitchen window, but it was raining. And our windows are hardly what you'd call clean at the best of times so I couldn't see clearly."

"Was it a man or a woman you saw?"

"I couldn't be sure. But I can tell you one thing - they were in a hurry."

When the police officers got back in their car, Dimbleby asked: "What do you make of her, Grace? I wouldn't mind betting she's spaced out - and probably she was back then as well."

"It's hard to say for sure, isn't it? But she seems to have seen someone."

"Did you pick up anything else, Grace?"

Grace grinned and flicked her curly dark hair. "Yes, one thing. That I've been wasting my time and money on expensive conditioners and shampoos when I could follow her example by just splashing on some blue and red dye!"

+++++

Livermore was receptive to what Dimbleby and Conteh had been told, but Nottage completely dismissive. He said: "Ruth Jenner can't be regarded as a reliable witness, Guv. Surely we're not going to reopen the case on the vague recollections of a druggie who admits she didn't have a clear view as it was raining? She's still heavily into drugs and may have been on a trip."

His boss considered the situation. "Yes, Miss

Jenner could have been spaced out, but we can't ignore her. What she has told Chris and Grace corresponds to what she said to Myra Thornhill so we must assume her recollection could be correct and she saw someone leaving by the back door of the crime scene. Whether or not that means this person had anything to do with Isabella Thornhill's death remains to be seen. But we need to follow it up."

"So do we reopen the case?" asked Dimbleby.

"Let's start by taking a more thorough look at a few people who had close connections with the Thornhills. We should start by talking to Hayden Stubbs, who Isabella reported for stalking her, and check out her brother-in-law Brandon Cunningham."

CHAPTER NINE

Wednesday, June 15th, 2022

Jeff Nottage recalled that Hayden Stubbs had been interviewed during the original investigation into Isabella Thornhill's death.

It had come to light that Stubbs had been charged with stalking Isabella 13 months previously. He'd been sentenced to 24 weeks' imprisonment, suspended for two years, and was issued with a five-year restraining order not to contact the victim.

Nottage and Conteh refreshed their memories by again reading the case history which showed that Stubbs had provided an alibi for the afternoon of the attack.

But the DI felt a pang of conscience as he drove with Conteh to Stubbs' pokey bedsit on the outskirts of Eastbourne.

'Perhaps we should have looked further into it,' he thought. 'Maybe I was too quick to accept that Thornhill was the killer.'

Nottage's mood was not improved by the belligerent attitude of the unkempt, unshaven and probably unwashed drop out.

"Why are you checking up on me?" asked Stubbs as he stood in bare feet on worn floorboards. "I haven't done anything."

Nottage tried to stay as far away from the smelly individual as possible as he told him: "Should we have any reason to believe you've misbehaved?"

"No. I've not been near another woman since I got done for stalking that model."

"Presumably you're referring to Isabella Thornhill. You no doubt recall being questioned by one of my colleagues after her death."

"Yeah, and I told you lot that I was drinking at my local when she was killed." Stubbs passed wind as he spoke and mumbled "sorry".

Nottage, forced to endure the unpleasant odour, replied: "So you did. It's the Swan and Duck, isn't it? And that's not far away from Mrs Thornhill's bungalow. It occurs to me that you could have left the pub, gone to Mrs Thornhill's home and got back before anyone noticed you were missing."

Stubbs became even more indignant. "That's a load of cobblers. I stuck to the restraining order and kept well away from her. But that didn't stop you lot hounding me after her death. You cost me my job - and it's because of you buggers that I'm in the sorry state I am now."

While Nottage took out a handkerchief from his pocket and blew his nose, Conteh asked: "How many women have you stalked, Mr Stubbs?"

"She was the only one."

"So why did you pick on Mrs Thornhill?"

"I recognised Isabella in the street after seeing a picture of her in a magazine. I followed her and tried to talk to her."

"But you didn't stop at that, did you? You returned to her home repeatedly and hung about outside. You also accosted her in the local shopping centre, shoved suggestive messages through her letter box and left her unwanted inappropriate presents. Did you take her a birthday present on the day she was killed?"

"No!" Stubbs said defiantly. "I bloody well didn't."

Nottage, who had been looking around the sparsely furnished room, now turned to face the man he found so objectionable. "The problem I have with believing you, Mr Stubbs, is what I can see on your wall. It's a picture of Isabella Thornhill in her underwear, isn't it?"

When they were outside Nottage told Conteh: "I think we both need sanitizing. That man stinks."

"I could tell he was getting up your nose," she joked.

Nottage smiled. "In every sense. Stubbs is a horrid individual and I have my doubts about him sticking to his court order. He became fanatical about Mrs Thornhill and was an annoying pest to her, but would he have been capable of committing an act of violence?"

Conteh's answer was not the one he was expecting. "There's no accounting for what men might be capable of doing if they allow their todger to do their thinking for them."

CHAPTER TEN

Wednesday, June 15th, 2022

Brandon Cunningham was a big, loud, boastful man who had made a fortune through shrewd investments and the occasional unscrupulous deal.

That had enabled him to buy himself the best of everything, including designer silk suits to hide his pot belly like the pale blue one he was wearing.

But the 45-year-old wheeler-dealer was worried that his latest shady transaction had been rumbled and would cost him his job as Chief Executive of cosmetics giant Soothing Products.

Cunningham had been heavily involved in price-fixing by entering into agreements with other companies to ensure their beauty treatments were not sold for less than the price specified by Soothing Products.

So when his secretary announced that the police wanted to see him, the businessman feared the worst.

"What can I do for you gentlemen?" he asked DS Michael O'Sullivan and DS Chris Dimbleby as they were shown into his office.

"We're looking further into the death of your

sister-in-law Isabella Thornhill and want to ask you a few questions," said O'Sullivan, taking a seat without being invited to do so.

Cunningham tried hard not to reveal either his relief or annoyance at what he considered to be a waste of his time.

"Fire away," he instructed.

"I gather she once worked for your company as a model on an advertising campaign," O'Sullivan began.

"Yes, she helped to promote some of our products."

"Did this involve her working closely with yourself?" inquired Dimbleby, sitting next to his colleague.

"Not really."

"But surely she accompanied you to events," the veteran copper persisted. "Were there many?"

"There were a few."

"And did you and Isabella become close?"

"I don't like what you're suggesting," snapped Cunningham, glaring at who he considered to be an impertinent, poorly dressed individual wearing a clearly un-ironed shirt.

"I'm not suggesting anything, sir. But as you raise the issue, was there any reason why we should think you had a relationship with Isabella?"

"Of course not. That's ridiculous and offensive - I'm happily married and so was Isabella."

"Not ridiculous when you consider that Isabella was an extremely attractive woman."

"Well, you've got it wrong."

"So, Mr Cunningham, you would have us believe that you're a perfect husband and you've never made a pass at any of the models you've worked with?"

The businessman's smirk gave him away.

O'Sullivan took over the questioning. "Did you have reason to visit Mrs Thornhill at her home?"

"Only when my wife and I went to see Isabella and George socially."

"And was that often?"

"Not really."

"Did you visit Mrs Thornhill on the day of her death?"

"No, I did not."

"Not to deliver a birthday present, perhaps?"

"No. I left it to my wife to send her something."

"And where were you on that day?"

"In the office."

"Presumably you went out for lunch?"

"I may have done. I don't recall."

"Strange that you don't recall where you were at the time your sister-in-law was killed," said O'Sullivan.

"Can you tell us if anyone else was very close to Mrs Thornhill, apart from her husband?"

"I don't think so." Cunningham was becoming fed up with these two tiresome policemen. "Why are you asking all these questions when George has already been convicted of killing her? Are you having second thoughts?"

O'Sullivan did not answer. Instead he probed further: "Did Mrs Thornhill have any enemies?"

"Not that I was aware of."

O'Sullivan rose. "Thank you for your time, Mr. Cunningham. We may wish to contact you again."

"Well if you do, perhaps you'll make an appointment. I'm an extremely busy man."

CHAPTER ELEVEN
Wednesday, June 15th, 2022

Livermore listened intently to what his team had to report about Cunningham and Stubbs.

"What's most interesting is the fact that the stalker still has a picture in his room of Isabella Thornhill. We need to recheck his alibi - Mike, can you speak to the landlord of the pub Stubbs insists he was in. Find out if he could have slipped out and come back unnoticed."

"Will do, Guv," the Irishman said.

"I'd also like to discover more about Cunningham. What do you make of this big wheeler dealer? Is he to be believed?"

O'Sullivan and Dimbleby had differing views. O'Sullivan's response was: "It's hard to accept Cunningham's claim that he can't remember where he was at the time of Isabella's death. But he was most insistent that they did not have an improper relationship. I'm inclined to believe him - she was probably out of his league."

Livermore turned to Dimbleby. "And what's your opinion, Chris?"

"I've just got a nasty feeling about him. He paints himself as Mr Clean, but he's probably a randy sod

- I could tell by the way he smirked when I asked him if he expected us to believe he never made a pass at any of the models working for him. I reckon that Cunningham's the sort of chancer who never gives up."

Livermore reflected that there was no evidence against Cunningham, but the words of Myra Thornhill rang in his head: "He's a womaniser and he had the hots for her."

"Let's probe deeper," the DCI said, looking across to DC Valerie Jones and PC Brian Hudson. "Valerie and Brian, can you talk to some of the staff at Soothing Products - those who came into contact regularly with both Cunningham and Mrs Thornhill while she did modelling there. And ask Cunningham's secretary to search through last year's diaries and computer records to see if they provide any clue as to where her boss was on the day in question."

Hudson gave a thumbs up sign and Jones said: "I'll have a woman-to-woman chat with the secretary and see if I can prise anything out of her."

Livermore also had an important task for Conteh. "Grace, I want you to go through all of Isabella's emails and phone calls. If any of you find anything at all connecting to Cunningham then Mike and Chris can pay him another visit. Let's put him under a bit of pressure."

Livermore waited for some murmurs in response before moving on. "We also need to keep a close eye on Hayden Stubbs. But he wasn't the only one giving Isabella grief. I've delved further into the case notes made prior to her husband's conviction and come up with the names Luke Newman and Harry Smithson. What can you tell me about them, Jeff?"

Nottage rubbed his chin thoughtfully. Newman and Smithson? Can you refresh my memory, Guv?"

"They were a couple of sex pests who targeted Isabella online. Presumably they picked on her because she was a model."

"Ah, yes. Both of them sent her explicit content on social media. We checked them out and found they were miles away at the time she was killed. One was near his home in the Midlands and the other in the North of England."

Livermore nodded. "What about Blodwen Knightly? The case notes say this so called lady put up some insulting messages on Facebook and Twitter about Isabella."

"That's right, Guv. She made several posts abusing Isabella. They were deeply offensive, but none of them threatening. The two women used to work together at a model agency in Brighton and there was apparently a clash of personalities. We came to the conclusion that Blodwen resented Isabella and was jealous of her, but not a physical threat."

Livermore nodded. "In light of what we've been told about someone leaving the crime scene, we should try to find out if Miss Knightly was anywhere in the vicinity that day. Jeff, perhaps you could have a chat with her and the head of the modelling agency. We need to know if Blodwen continued to hold a grudge against Isabella."

+++++

Only after arranging for his team to carry out a few more checks did Livermore put his boss in the picture, deciding it was best to take flack for something that he had already done than ask permission and risk being denied it.

Frampton seemed affable enough after inviting the DCI to take a seat in his spacious office and asked about his health. But the bonhomie did not last long.

Livermore wasn't surprised that his hypocritical senior officer voiced disapproval to the news he imparted.

"Harvey, I would have expected you to consult me before acting on this. While you were off sick our team found the evidence to convict George Thornhill for killing his wife. Everyone agreed it was an open-and-shut case. But now you're back you want to reopen it on the word of an unreliable witness who claims she saw someone leave the murder scene. The fact this witness is a known drug addict is worrying."

Livermore sighed and cracked his knuckles. "I haven't officially reopened the case, sir. I'm simply following up possible new evidence. I think you'll agree that we should do so in the interests of ensuring justice is carried out."

Frampton further expressed his concerns. "Obviously I want us to ensure that justice is done, but if this witness was hallucinating, we could be left with egg on our faces."

"With respect, sir, we could end up with more egg on our faces if we do not follow up this new lead and the Press subsequently find out about it"

"So what are you suggesting we do, Harvey?"

"We make inquiries to see if any other suspects emerge."

Frampton twirled his pen around in his right hand before answering. "Alright, Harvey. But make sure these 'inquiries' are carried out discreetly. And I expect to be kept posted on a daily basis. Is that understood?"

"Understood, sir. I'll keep it low-key."

CHAPTER TWELVE

Friday, June 17th, 2022

Once again Livermore found himself under pressure from not only his senior officer but his wife as well!

Evelyne caused him to be late leaving on Friday morning by emerging from her bedroom and yelling to him from the top of the stairs.

"You screeched, dear," he called back, not quite loudly enough for her to hear.

"Harvey, you told me you were going to ease yourself in gently at work following the cancer operation. But I've just listened to a message on our answerphone reminding you to keep your boss posted on any new developments about a killing. What's going on?"

"It's nothing to worry about, dear," he sighed. "Just a routine case."

"I don't believe you, Harvey," she retorted, coming down the stairs in a plain dressing gown that failed to conceal her waist which had increased in size considerably from the shapely young woman he'd married.

"I assure you there is nothing to worry about, darling. I'm taking things slowly and I'm feeling fine."

Evelyne was not to be fobbed off that easily. "Don't lie to me, Harvey. I've heard you gasping for breath at times. When you see the specialist I want to come as well so that I can make sure you do what he tells you."

"Let's talk about it later, dear," he suggested, reflecting that the deep love they once shared had given way to a protective companionship.

Evelyne was not finished. "Let me get you some breakfast before you go."

Harvey's mind flashed back to the soggy mess she'd made him the previous morning which turned out to be scrambled eggs. "I haven't got time, dear. I'll get something at work. Now give me one of your lovely smiles before I go."

Instead of accepting this attempt at a compliment, his fiery wife snapped: "Don't be so bloody sarcastic!"

Harvey thought it best to let his wife have the last word and contented himself with slamming the front door behind him.

+++++

Livermore was further delayed by a traffic diversion, and when he reached his office Nottage was waiting to see him.

"Take a seat, Jeff, and bring me up to date."

Nottage did as he was bid. "I've had words with Blodwen Knightly, Guv. She admits going completely over the top with her insulting posts about Isabella on Facebook and Twitter, but insists she never had any intention of taking things any further.

"She resented the decision made by the head of the model agency where they worked, Sally Hopper, that Isabella should replace her in a promotion for a swim wear company. Blodwen thought Isabella had touted for the job, and wanted to get back at her."

"And what does her boss say?"

"Sally Hopper told me Blodwen was absolutely furious. She kicked up such a fuss that Sally sacked her."

"Ah, Blodwen conveniently didn't tell you that, did she?" Livermore mused. "Getting the sack could have given her an even bigger grudge against Isabella. Can Blodwen account for where she was on the day Isabella was killed?"

"She says it was so long ago she can't remember, Guv. But she points out that she'd not contacted Isabella for some months and there was no reason to suddenly pop up on her birthday."

Livermore didn't fully accept that. "Maybe...or maybe she wanted to spoil Isabella's big day."

CHAPTER THIRTEEN
Friday, June 17th, 2022

DS Dimbleby, having taken a rare day off to get a dental bridge inserted where a front tooth had decayed, was not feeling at his best when he reported back on Friday.

He cursed that part of the bridge had a rough edge and his tongue kept scrapping against it. His discomfort became noticeable when he spoke which brought puzzled looks from Grace Conteh and Valerie Jones as he chatted with them upon his return.

"Are you alright, Chris?" inquired Grace in a concerned voice.

"Yes. I'm just suffering with this bloody bridge I've had fitted. Hopefully, I'll get used to the damned thing. It doesn't help that it's so stifling hot today. My mouth's drier than a camel's hindquarters in a sandstorm."

His joke did not get the laughs he expected, but Conteh was sympathetic. "It's expected to be the hottest day in the UK so far this year at over 30 centigrade. Let me get you a glass of water. And then we'll bring you up to date."

The brash O'Sullivan was not so polite. "What on

earth's the matter with you, mate?" he asked when Dimbleby tried to share with him the information he had obtained from Conteh and Jones.

"I've got a tooth problem," Dimbleby muttered. "It will probably be OK as I get used to this bridge. Never mind, me. I think we'd better go to see our old friend Cunningham again."

O'Sullivan did the talking when they arrived at Soothing Products and insisted that they see Cunningham.

When they were finally invited into his office Dimbleby's mumbled "Good morning" was greeted with a glare.

"I thought I told you to make an appointment?" the stern businessman challenged.

"We could always do this down at the station, if you prefer, sir," O'Sullivan replied, equally forcibly.

"OK, OK. What is it you want this time?"

O'Sullivan, who followed Dimbleby's lead in taking a seat, said: "We've had your office diary entries checked for the date Mrs Thornhill was killed and there's an unexplained absence concerning yourself, Mr Cunningham. Can you explain that?"

"Do you really expect me to remember what I was doing eight months ago?"

"Did you go to see Mrs Thornhill on her birthday?"

"No. Why on earth do you think I did?"

Dimbleby provided the answer. "Perhaps it's because you lied to us about your relationship with her. Our colleague has been looking at Isabella's emails and found one telling you that she could no longer work for you. She mentioned your 'inappropriate suggestions'."

Dimbleby, noting that Cunningham's brashness had seemed to disappear, pressed home the advantage he had gained. "Another email from Isabella asked you to no longer visit her at home."

There was a long silence. Finally the businessman admitted: "Alright, I did make the odd pass at her and on one occasion, after a few drinks, she seemed to be on the brink of letting me have my way. I took it as a sign she might be receptive if I tried my luck again. So I paid her a couple of visits. She turned me down and in the end I gave up."

This admission prompted O'Sullivan to demand: "Where were you on the day Isabella was killed? You must remember that."

Cunningham sighed and looked at both of them in turn. "Look, there are good reasons why I can't tell you. It could have the worst possible consequences for me."

"You mean with your wife?" Dimbleby asked,

removing his tongue from the sharp edge at the back of his bridge.

Cunningham scoffed. "You gentlemen apparently don't read the financial Press. Soothing Products has been charged with price-fixing by allegedly agreeing with two other companies to ensure that our cosmetics were not sold for less than a certain price. If we're found guilty I'll be forced to resign as Chief Executive."

Dimbleby was puzzled. "How does that explain where you were?"

The portly man looked distinctly uncomfortable. Eventually he came up with an answer. "Let me give you a hypothetical possibility. Suppose I was meeting an executive from one of the other two companies accused of price-fixing with us. If that came out, even if we were only talking about our golf handicaps, it would be disastrous."

"We will need the executive's name," said O'Sullivan.

"I can only give you that if it gets to the stage where you believe you have enough to charge me with Isabella's death," insisted the power broker. "But from what I've read about the case it seems pretty obvious to me that you have the right man already behind bars."

CHAPTER FOURTEEN

Friday, June 17th, 2022 to Monday, June 20th, 2022

Ruth Jenner found that drinking heavily at her local was most enjoyable, albeit not as satisfying as the euphoria which cannabis could give her.

She was now on her third gin and tonic while sitting near the back of the main bar of the Chalk and Cheese in Eastbourne with her mate Lynda, a younger version of herself, complete with tattoos, but with bright pink hair instead of red and blue.

Ruth was recounting to Lynda how the police had been questioning her.

"The bloody rozzers tried to put me away a couple of years ago," she was complaining. "Now the sods turn up out of the blue, wanting me to help them by recalling what I saw on the day Isabella Thornhill got herself topped."

"So what did you see?" asked Lynda, slurring her speech after consuming as much alcohol as her friend.

Ruth relished retelling her experience. "I looked out of our kitchen window and noticed someone leaving Isabella's place by the back gate - at least I thought I did."

"Aren't you sure?"

Grinning and flicking back her brightly coloured quiff, Ruth replied: "Pretty sure. But I was on a bit of a high that week after going to a coke party. You know how things can get a bit hazy sometimes."

"That's on a good day!" snapped Lynda. "I sometimes see strange objects and feel bugs crawling on me. Anyway, why are the police wanting to know about what you saw all those months ago?"

"I haven't the foggiest idea, love. It's a classic example of the fuzz wasting tax payers' money, isn't it, when they already have Isabella's husband locked up."

"Did you recognise who went out the back gate?"

"No. I only got a glance of them, and rain was pissing down, so I couldn't tell whether it was a bloke or a woman. And my head was buzzing. Anyway, let's talk about something more interesting, like getting our hands on some coke."

One person who found Ruth's recollections engrossing was sitting at the next table listening intently - local journalist Dougie Dudley.

He approached the two women and introduced himself. "I'm a reporter with the local paper. Perhaps I could buy you ladies a drink," he offered.

Ruth looked at him with the same disgust she

would show if treading on dog excrement. "Why don't you just F-off?" she hissed.

+++++

Dudley was undeterred, and wrote a story based on what he had just heard about a sighting of someone leaving the crime scene.

On Monday it appeared on the front page of the local Argus under the heading: NEW EVIDENCE IN KILLING OF MODEL.

This made unpleasant reading for Fussy Frampton. He called Livermore into his office and demanded: "Is this what you call conducting a low-key inquiry, Harvey?"

CHAPTER FIFTEEN
Tuesday, June 21st, 2022

Jennifer Duggan, who had become a big asset to Sussex Police's Public Relations team, knew all the guidelines, including the one that said she shouldn't engage in personal liaisons with journalists.

Yet here she was on her sofa next to local reporter Dougie Dudley after inviting him in for coffee following an enjoyable dinner together at the Thai restaurant down the road from her flat.

She'd had a few dealings with Dougie through her job, but it came as a surprise to the 28-year-old mousey blonde when he asked her out.

Jennifer rather fancied him so had gone to the trouble of wearing a smart pink satin shift dress and red high-heeled shoes.

The 'coffee' actually became a few glasses of wine, and Jennifer could no longer trust her judgement.

Now Dougie's goatee beard was brushing against her face as he kissed her on the cheek and then full on the lips.

Several kisses later he put his hand on her right knee and began to stroke her leg. As the kisses continued, Jennifer relaxed and allowed Dougie's hand to continue upwards.

She had experienced only a few sexual relationships and realised it would be unwise to let the obviously more active Dougie go too far too soon. "No," she whispered, but his gentle touch was proving irresistible.

As Dougie adjusted his position, Jennifer could feel his firmness pressing against her. Temptation got the better of her and she stroked the bulge.

Dougie groaned deeply, pushing her hand away briefly to unzip his flies. Her fingers went inside.

Feeling the excitement of the moment, Jennifer slid down her blue panties and things progressed swiftly. As he entered her, she cried out in ecstasy. After they had both been satisfied, they sat holding each other for several minutes.

"That was lovely," Jennifer said at length.

"Yes, it was fantastic," Dougie agreed. "We must meet up again soon. In the meantime, I might be phoning you in your official capacity in the Press Office tomorrow."

"Why's that?"

"I heard that your Major Crime Team has questioned a new witness regarding the death of Isabella Thornhill, even though her husband is serving time for killing her. Do you know anything about it?"

"No," she said, alarmed.

"Nothing at all?"

"No. But not everything goes through the Press Office."

"Well, I've already run a speculative story in the Argus about it. I did phone your Press Office, but I was right on deadline and the old cow I spoke to refused to make a comment. Now I'd like to write a follow up, with an official comment from the police. Perhaps you could look into it?"

"Is this why you asked me out?"

Jennifer could see from Dougie's facial expression that her suspicion seemed to be right. "Only partly," he said. "You're such a lovely person, Jen, and I want to go out with you again."

"Just because I'm a lovely person?"

"Don't be naïve, Jen - I adore your body, too!"

Her face reddened. "Well, I'd rather you didn't involve me in getting this story, Dougie."

"Alright. Who else can I speak to?"

"The person you referred to just now as an old cow. She's our senior Press Officer Stella Rudd and she'd be duty bound to look into it for you if you give her more time. But please don't mention that you know me personally. If Stella found out I was having...er...an affair with a journalist there would be hell to pay."

"Why? Surely you're entitled to see who you like outside the office."

"Now who's being naïve? Having a relationship with a journalist could be regarded as a conflict of interest."

"OK, keep your knickers on! Oh, I forgot, they're almost round your ankles, aren't they?"

"Don't be so naughty."

"Yes," he continued joking, "that was a bit below the belt, wasn't it."

"You really are unbelievable!"

"Thanks very much."

"I thought you were a journalist - not a comedian!"

"It's alright. I promise I won't mention you when I speak to Stella. She may be able to do an information swap with me."

"What do you mean?"

"Well, if the Major Crime Team is taking another look at the case I can give them a helping hand with a very useful tip off."

"Stella won't have the authority to do any sort of deal with you, Dougie."

"So who do you suggest?"

"Your best bet will probably be to ask her to pass on a message to the officer in charge of the Major Crime Team, DCI Harvey Livermore."

CHAPTER SIXTEEN

Wednesday, June 22nd, 2022

The next day, true to his word, Dougie Dudley did not mention Jennifer when he spoke to her boss about the Thornhill case.

He again got a frosty reception from a stern Ms Rudd. "I know nothing about this, Mr Dudley, and I'm not prepared to discuss it."

"Well," he replied, undaunted, "you might like to pass on a message to DCI Livermore. Would you please tell him that it would be mutually beneficial for him to speak to me about this. If he's taking another look at the case, I can give him some useful information."

+++++

Dougie was delighted to receive a phone call from Livermore within the hour.

"I understand you have some information for me, Mr Dudley," the police officer said.

"Yes, that's right, Chief Inspector. But what I'm proposing is that we actually do an exchange of information and you tell me why you're apparently looking into the Thornhill case."

"You seem to have been misled, Mr Dudley. I've no comment to make."

Undeterred, the journalist carried on. "I know that a witness saw someone leave the crime scene by the back door, Chief Inspector. I've already run a story on it."

"Yes, I saw it," snapped Livermore, sounding annoyed. "What you said was pure speculation and, as I've already told you, I've no comment."

Dougie persisted: "But if I provide you with some helpful information can you agree to give me the story exclusively when there's a development?"

"If you're able to tell me something useful, I'll probably show my appreciation," came the guarded reply.

"Alright, I take it we have a deal, Chief Inspector. You may be interested to know that George Thornhill was not the 'perfect' husband he claimed to be. He had an affair with a fellow employee called Raven Vickers."

"How do you know that?" Livermore said, sounding sceptical.

"I was given the information by a person who also used to work for Thornhill's development company. His name is Nigel Gray. He wouldn't agree to go on the record with me for a story, but I'm sure he'll give the police chapter and verse."

When Livermore dismissed this as "gossip", Dudley was ready with a convincing come back. "I think you'll find it all checks out. The woman with whom Thornhill was having the affair could even have been with him when he confronted his wife. Perhaps she was the person seen going out the back door."

CHAPTER SEVENTEEN

Wednesday, June 22nd, 2022

Nottage was called into Livermore's office to discuss Dougie Dudley's claims with his boss.

He was even more dubious than Livermore had been in his conversation with the journalist. "This reporter could be spinning us a yarn simply to get another story, Guv," he suggested.

"You may well be right, Jeff," conceded Livermore. "But, just as with Ruth Jenner, we need to follow up on it. I'd like you and Grace to track down Nigel Gray."

They found the developer on a building site in Bexhill and were able to talk to him in a small site office that Nottage felt was little bigger than a beach hut. But at least he and Conteh were able to sit on two fold-up chairs.

"We understand you used to work for Laleham Construction with George Thornhill," Nottage began.

"That's right," replied the affable forty-something man who was wearing a long sleeve check cotton lumberjack shirt despite the hot weather.

"And what did your job entail?"

"Much the same as I'm doing now in my present

job with Yardley and Bates. I was the contracts manager, working under George Thornhill. We carried out all sorts of building projects from offices to sports stadiums."

"Why did you leave?"

"George fired me."

Nottage, trying to make a note while peering though his glasses, only succeeded in unbalancing himself on the lightweight chair provided. He quickly adjusted his position. "Can you tell us why?"

"What's this all about, officer?" asked Gray, becoming less amiable.

Nottage gave the briefest of explanations: "We're just tidying up a couple of matters concerning the death of Mr Thornhill's wife. So why did he fire you?"

"Because his PA Raven Vickers accused me of racism. She alleged I made a racist comment about her being black - it was complete rubbish, and the truth of the matter was that she didn't like accepting instructions from me. But George took her word for it and sacked me."

"Just like that?" asked Conteh.

"Yes, just like that. I was in the process of taking out a case of unfair dismissal when George got banged up for killing his wife and the company shut down."

Nottage was content to let Conteh continue with the questioning while he made a further note. She encouraged the man to give a fuller explanation. "Why did Mr Thornhill accept the word of his PA against yours?"

"He was having an affair with her."

"What made you believe that, Mr Gray?"

"It became obvious. Their body language alerted me to it. Then I overheard a conversation between them which gave them away, and the clincher was when I saw George kissing her."

Tony Flood

CHAPTER EIGHTEEN

Wednesday, June 22nd, 2022

Livermore decided it was time he called a meeting of members of his Major Crime Team in the incident room at Lewes HQ to put things on a more official footing.

Those present included both uniformed and plain-clothed officers, Jennifer Duggan from Public Relations and crime analyst Helen Yates, whose use of software and data systems could reveal criminal trends and activities.

They seated themselves at workstations or on chairs in the large grey-carpeted room.

The DCI looked around at them and felt it was like old times, prior to recovering from his operation.

The supposedly hard copper allowed himself to indulge in a few moments of sentimentality as he watched Nottage straighten his glasses, Conteh cross one leg demurely over the other and Dimbleby exchange a wise-crack with O'Sullivan, who was sitting arrogantly on a desktop.

"OK," he called out at length. "Can everyone pay attention please. I have called this meeting to announce that I'm officially reopening the original 'Operation Butterfly'. We're going to delve deeper into the Isabella Thornhill killing following the sighting of someone leaving the crime scene."

"Does that mean we have reason to believe her husband didn't do it?" asked O'Sullivan.

"That remains to be seen, Mike. We're going to look at ALL possibilities, including that George Thornhill might have had an accomplice. It's been alleged he was having an affair with one of his employees, a lady called Raven Vickers. If this proves to be true we must ask ourselves whether Ms Vickers could have been at the crime scene with him. She may have been the person leaving by the back door."

"That's a bit of a long shot, isn't it, Guv?" Dimbleby suggested.

"Perhaps it is, Chris. But, as I've just said, we need to consider every possibility. An alternative scenario is that we convicted the wrong man and George Thornhill was telling the truth when he claimed he came home just after his wife was attacked."

This brought murmurs from most of those assembled and Livermore held up his right hand for silence. When it worked he could not prevent himself thinking 'I must try this at home with Evelyne.' He refocused and said: "So we should not rule out that someone else could have been the killer.

We have some potential suspects emerging including Isabella's former work-mate Blodwen Knightly, her brother-in-law Brandon Cunningham, and a stalker called Hayden Stubbs. But we need to keep an open mind on the whole situation."

This gave Nottage the chance to voice his reservations again. "Does that include the fact the only person who claims to have seen someone leaving the crime scene by the back door is a junkie?"

Livermore tried not to show any displeasure at being challenged, but could not prevent himself cracking his knuckles. "Yes, it does, Jeff. If this junkie, or Ruth Jenner as I prefer we call her, is right and we ignore her then we could be accused of suppressing relevant information."

"Sorry, Guv," Nottage apologised.

"OK, then Jeff. Your doubts have been noted, but we need to investigate every possibility, however unlikely it may appear. You and Grace can start by paying a visit to Raven Vickers. Let's see if she admits to having an affair with George Thornhill."

Livermore had one more piece of information to impart. "You should all note that, while I want us to examine everything with an open mind, I'd like us to initially conduct this on a low key basis."

He glanced at Jennifer Duggan and others in turn

as he added: "If anyone from the media asks you about the reopening of this case then I'd like you to give them a 'no comment' answer and inform me. Is that clear?" Livermore's tone hammered home that this was an instruction rather than a question.

CHAPTER NINETEEN
Wednesday, June 22nd, 2022

Nottage, accompanied by Conteh, felt they were fortunate to find Raven Vickers had just arrived home in her luxury apartment overlooking the sea in Eastbourne's Sovereign Harbour complex.

But she was far from welcoming, and Nottage took an instant dislike to this full-of-herself tall and shapely black American. She oozed sex appeal despite having her hair swept back into a bun. Not a single strand was out of place, but her near perfect appearance contrasted sharply with her abrupt manner.

"I don't want to talk about George Thornhill," she said bluntly.

"Well, we need you to do so in relation to a new line of inquiry we're following," replied Nottage.

"And what might that be?"

"I'm not at liberty to give you any details, madam. Now I'd like you to answer a few questions about the time you worked for Mr Thornhill at Laleham Construction."

Nottage had often been glared at before, but seldom with the contempt shown by Raven Vickers. Her dark brown eyes seemed to bore through him. "I've already told you I don't want to talk about him."

Nottage remained firm. "We can either do this here or at the station," he said.

"Alright, I'll answer your damn questions."

"How long did you work for Laleham Construction?"

"About four years."

"And did you become very close to Mr Thornhill during that time?"

"We had a good working relationship if that's what you mean."

"We understand it went beyond that, Ms Vickers, and you had an affair with him."

She spat out her answer: "How dare you make such a suggestion!"

Nottage was grateful Conteh stepped in to try to calm the enraged woman. "We have been given a statement to the contrary, Ms Vickers."

"Presumably from that low life Nigel Gray. He was sacked for racially abusing me so he's obviously got an axe to grind. You can't possibly believe anything he says about me or George."

Conteh stayed calm. "Look, Ms Vickers, we could find evidence to back this up by checking out hotels in which you and Mr Thornhill stayed etc. But surely it would be better for you if you confirmed it now."

"Of course George and I stayed at hotels together on occasions. I was his PA for goodness sakes. Don't you...!"

Nottage cut her short. "I think there's a good chance that if we contact some of those hotels we'll find you and Mr Thornhill shared a room. As DC Conteh says, it would be much easier for you to tell us what we want to know."

"OK, so we did have a relationship. So bloody what?"

Nottage exchanged a knowing look with his colleague before continuing. "Can you tell us, Ms Vickers, where you were on the day Isabella Thornhill was killed?"

"I've no idea!" retorted the still angry woman. "But I wasn't visiting her that's for sure. Why on earth would I do so?"

"Perhaps because you wanted Mr Thornhill to leave his wife for you and he refused," suggested Nottage. "You may have decided to bring matters to a head by telling her about your affair with her husband but things went badly wrong."

"Rubbish!" Vickers responded in a loud American twang.

Nottage, despite his limited knowledge of Shakespeare, found himself thinking of a famous line from Hamlet: 'The lady doth protest too much, methinks'.

CHAPTER TWENTY

Wednesday, June 22nd, 2022

Soon after Nottage and Conteh reported back, Livermore invited them to share the details of their vexatious meeting with other members of Operation Butterfly.

Nottage told them: "Raven Vickers is a most unpleasant person - aggressive, unhelpful and evasive and a liar to boot."

Dimbleby was quick to add: "Both the Thornhills had guilty secrets. The images of this blue-eyed couple were too good to be true."

Livermore summed up: "There seems to be a recurring theme here. We've found potential new suspects in Vickers, Cunningham and Hayden Stubbs. All three of them are being uncooperative and hostile. And all could be hiding something, as could Blodwen Knightly."

"Great minds think alike, Guv," Nottage agreed. "They're protesting a bit too much, aren't they?"

This brought a faint smile from his boss, pleased that his number two was finally seeing things his way. He turned to Valerie Jones and Brian Hudson. "I'd like you eagle-eyed pair to study CCTV and ANPR records in the vicinity of the

Thornhills' home to see if there were sightings of these people, or their cars, on the day of Isabella's death."

"I've already started with the CCTV," Jones told him. "So perhaps I can continue that while Brian begins taking a look at what the ANPR system has got regarding number plate recognition."

Livermore nodded. "It's a long, monotonous business so I'll assign a couple of others to help you. It could prove rewarding. See if you can dig anything up."

When the team meeting ended, Livermore decided to play it safe and bring his boss up to date.

For once he was not kept waiting and, upon entering Fussy's office, guessed from his boss's body language that the man was impatient to get home.

Livermore lost no time in relaying the latest information about the investigation and quite enjoyed seeing Frampton's shocked reaction.

"So, Harvey, you're suggesting we may have three suspects in a stalker, a brother-in-law and a lover? Oh, and there's also a model who may have had an axe to grind."

"Well, it's a possibility, sir. The stalker, the brother-in-law and the model were questioned as part of the original investigation soon after the attack on Mrs Thornhill took place, but Raven Vickers has only just come to light. Even Nottage, who was instrumental in getting Thornhill convicted, concedes Vickers may have gone to see his wife in an attempt to break up the marriage. The two women could have had a row which ended in Isabella being stabbed. Perhaps she was already dying when George arrived home."

Frampton shook his head.

"Of course, there is another scenario, sir."

"Which is?"

"We now know George Thornhill was having an affair and was therefore not the perfect husband he tried to make himself out to be. This, of course, gave him a possible motive to kill his wife, didn't it?"

Livermore inhaled before continuing: "Perhaps he and Raven Vickers both confronted Isabella. He could still have done the stabbing, and maybe Vickers was the person seen leaving the crime scene by the back door."

Frampton's mouth dropped slightly open. But instead of finding this suggestion far fetched as Dimbleby had done, he welcomed it.

"So if that's how it went down we've already convicted the right man. We now need to find the evidence to lock up his accomplice as well."

Tony Flood

CHAPTER TWENTY-ONE
Thursday, June 23rd, 2022

Harvey Livermore was horrified when his wife Evelyne insisted on coming with him for his hospital appointment as part of the check ups following his lung operation.

"Be reasonable, dear," he protested. "This is my chance to talk about any concerns I might have and seek reassurances to hopefully give me peace of mind. It will be difficult for me to do so if you're with me."

"Nonsense, Harvey!" her Scottish voice chastised him. "I want to know the results of the scans you've had and the full up-to-date situation. I can't trust you to tell me everything, can I?"

Her husband cracked his knuckles in frustration.

As Harvey had feared, his appointment with Dr Morgan in respiratory medicine was dominated by his wife.

The doctor started by informing the Livermores that everything was going well.

He was his usual charming self and did not seem concerned about Evelyne asking him far more questions than his patient.

"What symptoms should we look out for?

Will Harvey have any on-going health issues? What can he do to minimise these? What is the chance of any infection returning?"

Harvey was relieved that Dr Morgan was prepared to answer all these points, which he had been intending to ask himself.

When Evelyne paused briefly, the doctor smiled, rubbed the designer stubble on his chin, and told Harvey: "You may continue to get tired and struggle for breath at times, but do the exercises and you should be OK."

Evelyne then launched into a stream of additional concerns. "Harvey's still drinking whisky and refusing to stick to a balanced diet. And I've given up trying to encourage him to come for walks with me."

The normally unruffled policeman cringed.

"Is this true, Mr. Livermore?"

"I do like the occasional whisky, doctor, and I get fed up eating fruits and vegetables. Surely, having fish and chips or curry once in a while isn't going to do any harm."

Dr Morgan conceded: "While it's important, Mr Livermore, that you follow the diet provided by the nutritionist, giving yourself the odd 'treat' is acceptable. It might help if you do go for walks with your wife."

Harvey groaned inwardly as a beaming Evelyne announced in a firm Scottish voice: "Aye, that's what we'll do."

Dr Morgan confirmed: "It might improve both your fitness and breathing, Mr Livermore. How are your bowl movements and sexual functions?"

Evelyne almost exploded with indignation. "What sexual functions? If he's performing any they certainly aren't with me!"

The doctor concluded the check up by saying: "If you wish, I can recommend a therapist to provide sessions dealing with causing stress to your partner."

Evelyne was quick to respond. "There, Harvey. These sessions are just what you need."

No," the doctor corrected. "They would be for you, Mrs Livermore."

CHAPTER TWENTY-TWO
Thursday, June 23rd, 2022

Livermore called a late morning meeting of Operation Butterfly and asked if any of the team had come up with new leads. He was delighted when Conteh obliged.

The bright young Senegalese officer announced that she had contacted Raven Vickers' bank and been shown copies of her statements going back two years.

"I found two of the payments most revealing," she said. "Ms Vickers made them to an abortion clinic earlier this year."

"So Thornhill got her banged up!" said Dimbleby crudely.

Conteh joined her boss in frowning at their colleague who seemed oblivious to his crassness. She acknowledged Dimbleby's observation by adding: "That would appear to be the case. Immediately after Vickers had made these payments to the abortion clinic, her account was credited with two transfers for exactly the same amounts."

"From George Thornhill's account?" asked Livermore.

"No, but from his company Laleham Construction, and they were signed by him."

This prompted Livermore's rugged features to register one of his unaccustomed broad smiles. "Great work, Grace," he beamed.

Dimbleby, who Livermore noticed had been licking the back of his front tooth, gave his view. "This is as good as an admission that Thornhill was the father. Why else would he authorise his company to pay for the abortion?"

O'Sullivan was sceptical, however. "I don't see how it takes things much further. Surely getting rid of the baby would have let Thornhill off the hook. Neither he nor his mistress would then have a reason to kill his wife, would they?"

Livermore rubbed his stubbly chin as he considered this theory. "You may be right, Mike. But if the affair continued, Ms Vickers might have become convinced she could persuade Thornhill to leave his wife for her. She could have decided to up the ante by confronting Isabella on her birthday. Perhaps she did so before Thornhill got home."

Nottage rose to his feet. "I think Grace and I should have another talk with Ms Vickers."

+++++

Soon after the meeting ended Livermore received a telephone call from George Thornhill's sister Myra.

"Have you followed up on the information I gave you, Chief Inspector?" she wanted to know.

"We're still in the process of doing so, Ms Thornhill. But I'm not able to discuss an on-going investigation with you, I'm afraid."

Myra's voice shot up a couple of decibels. "Please don't fob me off. I'm entitled to know if you've questioned the neighbour who saw someone leave the crime scene by the back door. Or should I go and ask her myself?"

Livermore sighed. "We've spoken to a new witness, and as a result we are considering other possible outcomes."

"And have you questioned Isabella's stalker and her brother-in-law Brandon Cunningham?"

"We're speaking to various people, but I cannot possibly divulge their names. Now, let me ask you a question, Ms Thornhill. Were you aware that your brother was having an affair?"

"What!" bellowed Myra down the phone, causing Livermore to rub his ear. "There's no way George would have been unfaithful to Isabella - he loved her to bits."

The policeman tactfully pointed out: "Men have

been known to love their wives and still have an affair with another woman."

"Well, I can't believe George would have done that. Presumably, you're talking about his stuck up PA Raven. I could tell she fancied him, but I'm sure he wouldn't have succumbed to any temptations she provided. If he did he was a fool."

This gave Livermore cause to ponder: 'Yes, George Thornhill had been a fool - but just how big a fool?'

FALL GUY

PART THREE

CHAPTER TWENTY-THREE
Thursday, June 23rd, 2022

When Nottage and Conteh arrived outside Raven Vickers' apartment she was in her Hyundai Tucson, about to leave.

Nottage, hearing her reviving up, jumped out of his unmarked BMW, which he had parked a few yards away. He ran towards the Hyundai, and signalled it to stop.

But to his complete surprise Vickers seemed even more intent on departing.

She swung her car out backwards and, despite the policeman's efforts to take evasive action, the Hyundai hit him hard on the lower part of the body.

Nottage yelled in agony and went down on the ground in a heap.

He remained conscious and was aware of Conteh running to his aid as the BWM drove off.

+++++

Nottage found himself in a bed in Eastbourne Hospital. He was no longer in agony due to medication and painkillers.

When his wife Kim arrived, he experienced some

of the excessive attention from a spouse that his boss Livermore had received on a regular basis since his operation.

A short time later an Indian doctor appeared and spoke to them both.

"I'm Dr. Mamood. The X-rays and tests we've done show you have suffered a pelvic fracture. It's not severe, but we need to check there is no other damage."

"What sort of damage?" Kim wanted to know.

"Yes, please give us the worse case scenario, doctor," said the anxious patient.

"Well, after being struck by a car in this manner, there could be injuries to organs within the pelvic ring such as the intestines, kidneys, bladder or genitals."

"That sounds pretty serious, doctor," Nottage groaned.

"I think it's unlikely to be the case with you, but we need to make sure. Hopefully, you've escaped with a minor fracture that can be treated with bed rest and medication."

"Do you hear that, Inspector Clouseau?" Kim said sarcastically, her pretty freckled face forming a big grin. "You're being confined to bed - you're off the case!"

Nottage was pleased that the doctor's

reassurance caused Kim to stop fussing, and she was content to simply hold his hand.

Visits from Conteh and Livermore followed. They filled their colleague in with what had happened to Raven Vickers. Her car had soon been spotted, leading to her being taken to Eastbourne nick, where she was initially charged with failing to stop at the scene of an accident.

"What about doing her for trying to kill me?" Nottage asked.

Livermore's answer placated him. "I don't think we can go that far, Jeff, but she won't be driving again for a long time. That could be the least of her worries if we find she was involved in the death of Isabella Thornhill."

CHAPTER TWENTY-FOUR
Thursday, June 23rd, 2022

Livermore asked Dimbleby to assist him in questioning Raven Vickers at Eastbourne Custody Suite.

She had called upon one of Sussex's most respected solicitors, Lawrence Petterson, to represent her, but she set the tone in the stark interview room by being uncooperative and belligerent, while defiantly admitting to nothing.

Livermore showed his annoyance, cracking his knuckles loudly. "Because of you, Ms Vickers, a police officer is in hospital with a serious injury. Does it ever occur to you that you are in the wrong?"

"I can't actually recall an occasion when it has, Chief Inspector," she retorted sarcastically.

"Let me give you some advice, Ms Vickers. You are not helping yourself. You could come up on causing serious injury by careless driving as well as failing to stop and failing to report a road traffic accident. This may result in a prison sentence. Then there's your possible involvement in the murder of Mrs Thornhill. It might help if you cooperate which has not been the case so far.

Now are you going to answer our questions properly?"

He met her glare full on until she turned away on the opposite side of the table from him to whisper into the ear of her solicitor.

Livermore soon discovered that whatever words of wisdom the high-charging Lawrence Petterson might have uttered went unheeded because her attitude remained frosty. "As I've already stated, I did not mean to hit the policeman with my car. I only did so because he ran into my path and I didn't see him. It was an accident. You're just bluffing."

Livermore cracked his knuckles again and said: "I don't bluff. Raven Vickers, I am charging you with..."

"Alright!" she snapped. "Ask your damn questions."

The DCI looked at his notes and told her: "I want to discuss your relationship with George Thornhill prior to the death of his wife. We have copies of your bank statements showing that you made two payments to an abortion clinic. Was this to terminate your pregnancy."

"Yes."

"And was George Thornhill the father?"

"I prefer not to say."

"Don't play games, Ms Vickers. Your bank

statements also show you received two payments from Mr Thornhill's company that were identical sums to the amounts you paid for the abortion."

"OK, George was the father."

"What was the reason for you terminating the pregnancy?"

Vickers crossed one shapely leg over the other and took her time replying. "I wasn't into playing happy families."

"Can you expand on that, Ms Vickers?"

"I've nothing further to say."

Dimbleby turned to his boss but spoke loudly enough for Vickers to hear: "Why don't we just charge her with wasting police time, Guv?"

Petterson, a man in his fifties with slicked back hair, responded sharply: "Is that meant to intimidate my client?"

"No," replied Livermore firmly. "I agree with my colleague. If your client is going to persist in this unhelpful, time-wasting manner then that is what we will do."

Vickers' attitude suddenly changed. "OK. There were two reasons for the termination. One was because, as a career woman, it did not suit me to have a baby. The second was that George encouraged me to do so...he didn't want to risk his marriage at that stage."

"Yet you were prepared to carry on your relationship with him?"

"Why not? We were having great sex, and I believed it would be only a matter of time before he left Isabella for me."

Livermore pressed further. "But that never happened, did it? So did you decide to bring matters to a head and pay Isabella a visit? And for maximum impact do so on her birthday?"

Vickers seemed to become ruffled for the first time. "That's complete nonsense. I never went near her."

"Can you prove it?" challenged Dimbleby.

The solicitor intervened. "It's not up to my client to prove she didn't confront Mrs Thornhill - it's up to you to show she did. And that's not possible because it never happened."

Livermore changed tact. "What's been your relationship with George Thornhill since he was charged? Have you visited him in prison?"

"No I haven't. There's no longer a relationship."

"But I thought I loved him? I would have expected you to show your loyalty in his time of need."

Vickers shook her head mockingly. "You obviously know nothing about me, Chief Inspector. In my book loyalty goes out of the window when your lover turns out to be a killer."

Livermore showed his surprise. "Didn't you believe his claims that he never did it?"

"You didn't and the jury didn't so why should I? There's no way I would wait for a killer to come out of jail and risk being his next victim. I want nothing more to do with him."

Livermore shook his head, but wanted to know whether her own experiences with Thornhill justified her feeling this way. "Were there any occasions when you saw him lose his temper?"

"You mean to the extent he could knife someone? Only once. That was when he wanted to show off his culinary skills and spent hours cooking me a special goulash dish. I took one taste and told him it was crap. He became so angry he picked up my plate and threw it against the wall."

Tony Flood

CHAPTER TWENTY-FIVE

Friday, June 24th, 2022

Livermore again cast his mind over the suspects who had emerged and wondered if any of them could be believed.

His thoughts were interrupted by Dimbleby bursting into his office after the briefest of knocks.

"Do come in, Chris," he chided.

"Sorry, Guv. Have you seen the financial Press today?"

"Can't say I have Chris. What have you read that you're so excited about?"

"Brandon Cunningham has received his comeuppance. His company Soothing Products has been fined £4.5 million for price fixing and Cunningham's resigned as Chief Executive."

"That's very interesting," mused Livermore. "But his financial fiddlings coming to light don't help us with the Isabella Thornhill case do they?"

"They might, Guv. Now he's had to quit, Cunningham may be willing to name the executive from the rival company he was supposedly meeting in secret on the day of the killing. We might find out whether or not he had an alibi."

"Good thinking, Chris. OK. Why don't you add to

his woes by having another talk to him?"

"Will do, Guv. It's awful when a high flyer gets knocked off his perch, isn't it?"

+++++

Later that day Livermore called another meeting of Operation Butterfly. Apart from Nottage, a few others were missing due to Covid and holidays, and the atmosphere felt a bit flat.

"Have any of you got some more news for me?" the DCI asked.

Dimbleby was the first to speak. "Brandon Cunningham has gone to ground after being forced to resign as Chief Executive of Soothing Products for price fixing. There's no sign of him at his office or at his home, and his wife claims he's being questioned by the fraud squad. So we might have to wait until Monday to speak to him."

Livermore turned to Helen Yates and asked the analyst: "Have you uncovered much about Cunningham's activities, Helen?"

"I've got full details about the price fixing, Guv. They're all here," the twenty-something redhead replied, passing him a file. "Soothing Products and other companies conspired to sell some of their cosmetic ranges at the highest possible retail prices to increase profits. I'm now looking deeper into Cunningham's financial dealings, and I'll try to find out if there are likely to be any further charges to follow."

Mike O'Sullivan was the next to speak. "I've been to the Golden Goose pub where Haydon Stubbs' alibi was that he was drinking all afternoon. The landlord, Richard Wilkes, says Stubbs has let himself go badly and has been barred. But he was a regular prior to losing his job, and Mr Wilkes recalls serving him drinks and a lunch on the day Mrs Thornhill was killed. But he can't swear that Stubbs didn't slip out at some stage and then return."

"Does the landlord have any idea how long Stubbs could have gone missing without him noticing?"

O'Sullivan checked in his notebook. "His exact words were: 'Do me a favour. How the bloody hell do you expect me to remember that?'."

"Hmm," Livermore muttered. "Well, it's an alibi of sorts, but not conclusive. Anyone else got anything?"

Valerie Jones raised her hand.

"Yes, Valerie."

"Unfortunately, Guv, neither the CCTV nor ANPR systems have shown our suspects, or their cars, in adjoining roads to the Thornhills' home on the day Isabella was killed. But what we have discovered is that Raven Vickers and Blodwen Knightly were both actually parked in shopping centres at the relevant time, and these two centres were within walking distance of the crime scene."

"That's a good point, Valerie. We need to follow up on that."

Dimbleby offered his opinion. "Either Vickers or Knightly might have thought they'd pay a surprise visit to Isabella to ruin her birthday. Perhaps they've been telling us a pack of lies. And Vickers is certainly cold blooded enough to be a killer."

+++++

Dimbleby repeated his thoughts about Raven Vickers having a killer's mentality to Nottage when he visited him in hospital with a bag of grapes that evening.

"Too true," said Nottage, putting to one side the grapes his colleague had thrust into his hand. "I'm convinced that bitch drove her car at me on purpose."

"Well, she'll be coming up on multiple charges so she could be joining her ex-lover Thornhill in the nick. Anyway, how are you getting on, Jeff?"

"Fine, thanks Chris. The doctors say my injury isn't serious and I should be out of here tomorrow. But I've got to take it easy for a few weeks. Are they bringing anyone in as a temporary replacement for me?"

"That's unlikely, mate, with staff shortages and Covid. If they do, they won't find anyone better than you - unless they come up with a mini-skirted nymphomaniac!"

Nottage grinned at the crude joke. "Don't try to make me laugh, you bastard. It will hurt like mad. Surely our team must be under-staffed."

"Yes, we are. It didn't help when we had to look into a possible kidnapping which turned out to be a false alarm after a young boy decided to get on a bus by himself instead of waiting for his mother. But, apart from that, we've been fully focused on the killing. So we're working flat out while you're lazing around in bed."

Nottage again feigned a smile. "Perhaps you should be getting back to the office, then, Chris."

CHAPTER TWENTY-SIX

Friday, June 24th, 2022 and Saturday, June 25th, 2022

Livermore reread some of the original case notes, including a statement taken by Conteh from Isabella's best friend Carlotta Agostini back in October last year.

He was surprised to see that Conteh was still at her desk and asked her what she remembered about Carlotta.

"She was extremely distressed about her friend's death and kept breaking down crying so it was rather difficult to get a lengthy statement, Guv."

"I'd like you to speak to her again, Grace. In the light of the new evidence we're considering, it might be helpful if Carlotta gives us a bigger insight into Isabella and the people she had come into contact with. Find out if Carlotta knew much about Brandon Cunningham, Raven Vickers and Blodwen Knightly. And was she aware whether the stalker bothered Isabella again?"

+++++

Grace recalled that Carlotta Agostini worked as a massage therapist so she phoned on Saturday morning and arranged to see her during a one-hour gap in the Italian woman's busy schedule at 2pm.

After exchanging brief pleasantries in the treatment room of Carlotta's clinic, which consisted of a treatment table, a desk, two chairs and shelves filled with books, Grace explained the purpose of her visit.

"So what more can you tell me about Isabella Thornhill and your friendship with her?"

The therapist's oval face lit up as she reflected. "We both had Italian roots and formed a close bond together. She was a lovely person who seldom had a bad word to say about anybody."

Grace was quick to pick up on that. "And on those few occasions when she did have cause to do so, who would those bad words have been directed at?"

"Well, we both called Blodwen Knightly a few choice names over the vile posts she made about Issie on Facebook. Some of the awful things that woman said were libellous. That's why Issie complained to Facebook, causing them to take appropriate action and block Blodwen."

"Do you think the bad feeling between the two

women could have resulted in Blodwen seeking Isabella out and trying to wreck her birthday?"

"You mean could she have stabbed Issie? I never met Blodwen so I wouldn't know what she was capable of doing. I think a more likely suspect would be the stalker."

"Hayden Stubbs?"

"Yes. Even after the court order issued against him, Issie was terrified he might return."

"And did he?"

"Issie saw him on one occasion when she was sitting in a coffee bar waiting for me. He hung around outside, but eventually went away and, as far as I know, she never saw him again."

"How long was that before her death?"

"Probably only a month or so."

Conteh accepted the offer of a drink and continued her questioning. "What about Brandon Cunningham and Raven Vickers? Do you know anything about them?"

"Yes. Issie and George gave out my business cards to lots of people they knew, and that led to Brandon and Raven coming to me for massages. I found both of them to be unpleasant. Brandon made me feel uncomfortable by asking if I did 'extras' and then giving me the silent treatment when I said 'no'."

"And what about Raven?"

"She turned up more than an hour late for her appointment. When I told her I would only be able to give her a 30-minute treatment instead of the one hour she had booked because I had another client coming soon, she went into a hissy fit and stormed off."

Conteh made notes and then asked: "As a model, did Isabella often receive unwanted attentions from men that might have upset her?"

"Yes. She told me it was the downside of being an attractive woman. Isabella had to put up with sex pests sending her inappropriate messages through social media. Men she met at various functions would also come on to her - even those who knew she was married. A few seemed to become infatuated with her, or perhaps they were just trying to bed a model."

"And how did she cope with this?"

"She found some of these jerks a real pain, but managed to turn most of her admirers down without any bad feeling. She even enjoyed flirting if it was nothing more than friendly banter."

Conteh scribbled frantically in her note book. "Did she ever succumb to these advances?"

"Isabella told me that on one occasion, after a few drinks, she almost responded, but insisted she never had sex with another man since marrying George."

Conteh wanted to know more. "Did she give you any details of those occasions when guys took offence at being turned down? Or were too persistent?"

The amiable policewoman waited patiently to give Carlotta time to reflect. "Issie did admit that some situations frightened her. She told me about her vulnerable side in one of our chats over coffee after going to the gym together. You see, she'd been raped as a teenager and this left her traumatised."

"How awful," Conteh acknowledged.

"Yes, Issie told me her attacker also taunted her. When she tried to cover up after he ripped her bra and exposed her breasts, he said she was a prick tease. Then the brute raped her."

Conteh made eye contact with Carlotta and nodded, encouraging her to continue.

"Issie was mortified. She said the bastard repeated 'that will teach you to be a prick tease' while he was having his way with her. She felt completely degraded. For several years she did not have any proper relationships with men. But Issie was able to do so in her twenties, and had sexual liaisons with a couple of serious boy friends before she met George."

Conteh felt it was vital to clarify one last point. "Did Isabella give you any names of those men who tried their luck with her while she was married?"

"Not really, although she hinted that her brother-in-law fancied her like mad. But you're forgetting about the women, aren't you?"

"What do you mean?" asked Conteh.

"Whenever Issie entered a room she not only received admiring glances from most of the men, but also scowls from some of the women. Wives and partners were jealous and resentful of the attention she received. She could tell that those ladies clearly did not like her - some probably hated her."

CHAPTER TWENTY-SEVEN
Monday, June 27th, 2022

Conteh relayed all the information that Carlotta had given her to the next meeting of Operation Butterfly.

She was rewarded with a beam from Livermore. "You've done well to find out so much, Grace. It helps paint a very good picture of both Isabella, how vulnerable she was, and some of those who came into contact with her."

"Yes," added O'Sullivan. "We now know that Hayden Stubbs was probably continuing to stalk her. And we've got confirmation that Brandon Cunningham and Raven Vickers are both the sort of repulsive people you'd want to avoid at all costs."

"But not necessarily killers," Livermore reminded him. "I'm trying to keep an open mind on the whole case. There are three options for us to consider. Option One is that Thornhill killed his wife; Option Two, he attacked her with the aid of someone else; or Option Three, like Thornhill's insisted all along, he found her after someone else had done it."

Dimbleby gave his opinion. "If he had an accomplice it must have been that arrogant cow Raven Vickers. They could have told Isabella about their affair and it all got out of hand."

"Maybe," mused Livermore. "But what if Thornhill had nothing to do with it?"

Dimbleby did not hesitate to use black humour to lighten the atmosphere. "If Thornhill's innocent then I'd make Hayden Stubbs the 2-1 favourite, with Brandon Cunningham and Raven Vickers 3-1 shots and Blodwen Knightly the 10-1 outsider."

This prompted Brian Hudson to pipe up: "If you're taking bets, Chris, I'll have a fiver on Vickers doing it."

While Livermore was calling for order, he noticed that Valerie Jones had answered a call on her mobile and was trying to attract his attention.

"Yes, Valerie? Have you got some good news for me?"

"I have indeed, Guv. That was Cunningham's secretary, Priscilla Miller. She's been able to tell me where he was at the time Mrs Thornhill was killed."

"How's that possible, Valerie?"

"The diary Priscilla had showed me simply said Cunningham was out for lunch. But she mentioned that all their company cars have trackers. She can look them up on a computerized tracker system to see if salesmen are where they're supposed to be."

"And was she able to locate Cunningham?"

Valerie gave a big grin. "Yes, Guv. His BMW was in a car park for almost two hours, just a short walk from Isabella's home."

"Blimey!" exclaimed Chris.

Valerie continued: "Priscilla says Cunningham hasn't been in the office today following his resignation, but she thinks he's at home."

Livermore was delighted. "Great work, Valerie. I think Chris and Mike should pay him a home visit - I'm sure he'll welcome you both as old friends. Ring me if you come up with anything."

+++++

Livermore received a phone call from Dimbleby sooner than he had expected.

"Brace yourself for a shock, Guv," said his longest serving officer. "Brandon Cunningham has committed suicide."

"Are you sure it's suicide, Chris?"

"There can be little doubt, Guv. Mike and I are at his penthouse where his wife Anna found him dead in the lounge upon returning from a hair dressing appointment. There's an empty bottle of antidepressants on a table next to the body, together with a note which could be interpreted as a confession that he killed Isabella Thornhill."

Livermore gasped in surprise. "Read it to me."

Dimbleby did as he was asked. It says: 'To my darling Anna. I'm so sorry. The price fixing has ruined me and a lot worse will follow soon when it comes out about IT. It's too much. I can't go on. Please forgive me. All my love, Brandon'."

Livermore asked Dimbleby to repeat it and considered the wording carefully. "This reference to 'IT' seems to be an admission that he killed Isabella Thornhill, or maybe it simply refers to the shame of being exposed as a sex pest. Anyway, it's pretty conclusive he committed suicide, Chris. But let's play safe and call SOCO in."

"I've already done so, Guv. But we may never find out for sure if he killed his sister-in-law, will we?"

CHAPTER TWENTY-EIGHT
Monday, June 27th, 2022

Donal McCarthy was making the most of his day off from Express Couriers.

The podgy, balding delivery man was sprawled out on the armchair in his cramped lounge, drinking larger from a can and watching the opening day of Wimbledon tennis on TV.

To be more precise he was looking solely at the women's singles and focusing on the attractive scantily-clad contestants who were turning him on.

It saddened him to see one young hopeful getting beaten. 'It's a great shame I won't see much more of her,' he thought. 'She's got great legs and a lovely little arse.'

When the teenager scampered in vain to reach a full blooded cross-court shot, McCarthy's right eye began to twitch excitedly as he marvelled at her daring outfit which clearly showed she was braless and wearing dazzling white panties.

The match finished too early for McCarthy's liking. He discarded the larger to light a cigarette, and his mind reflected on some of the sexy women he had encountered.

'That bloody tart who accused me of touching her up three years ago was really something,' he mused. 'Then there was that tasty little number I used to look at through her bedroom window. But neither of them were as hot as Isabella whatshername. She looked fantastic in a black kimono that barely covered her tits. What a bloody laugh that the cops only wanted to interview me as a witness'.

He decided it was time to give himself a treat, and what better way to do it, he thought, than look through the girlie magazine he had bought that day, showing women scantily dressed or completely nude in a variety of erotic poses.

CHAPTER TWENTY-NINE
Tuesday, June 28th, 2022

Helen Yates was a few minutes late arriving for the mid-morning meeting of Operation Butterfly and found that Livermore was filling the team in on Brandon Cunningham's suicide.

"The bottle of empty pills and the note in his hand writing confirm that Cunningham took his own life," her boss was saying. "Where the note refers to 'the price fixing has ruined me and a lot worse will follow soon when it comes out about IT' could be an admission he killed Isabella Thornhill."

Yates put up her hand to speak and did so without waiting to be asked. "I don't think 'IT' was referring to Isabella Thornhill, Guv."

"And why's that, Helen? What have you found out?"

She gave Livermore a toothy grin before answering. "I've been looking at the latest news feeds and data. It's emerged that Brandon Cunningham was notified shortly before he committed suicide that he was to face further charges of fraud. He'd been involved in insider trading by selling shares prior to releasing adverse business performance reports, and also evaded more than £200,000 in income tax. He was almost certainly going to prison."

Yates waited a few seconds before delivering her punch line. "So the initials 'IT' were more likely to stand for either 'Insider Trading' or 'Income Tax."

Livermore was among those to show their surprise.

Dimbleby became the first to respond. "Yeah, you're probably right, Helen. The likelihood of a long stretch in the nick for fraud could have been the final straw for Cunningham. He had taken a few risks too many."

Yates responded. "Cunningham's other fraudulent activities only came to light after Soothing Products were investigated for price-fixing."

O'Sullivan for once concurred with his old sparring partner Dimbleby. "It seems all Cunningham's scams were being uncovered at the same time, so even a hard-nosed businessman like him probably found it too much to take."

Livermore also agreed. "It does sound the more obvious reason for his suicide. But, even so, he can't be ruled out as Isabella Thornhill's possible attacker. Unfortunately, we can no longer check whether he was telling the truth about having an undercover meeting in a car park with an executive from a rival company at the time Isabella was killed."

The DCI looked around for any other opinions. Dimbleby came up with one after he had finished running his tongue around his troublesome dental work. "Of course, Guv, Cunningham had time to do both."

"Sorry, Chris? What do you mean?"

"His car was parked for almost two hours, wasn't it? There was enough time for him to have a clandestine meeting in the car park and still visit Isabella. His mobile phone data would not have shown where he went if he left the phone in his car and walked to Isabella's bungalow."

Livermore actually gave his colleague a clap. "Take a bow, Chris. That's a possibility I hadn't considered. We need to make every possible check. Let's go through all Cunningham's emails, telephone calls - everything."

CHAPTER THIRTY

Wednesday, June 29th, 2022

Livermore ignored a phone call from Dougie Dudley, but answered when the persistent journalist rang for the third time.

"What can I do for you, Mr Dudley?" he asked cautiously.

"I'd like to know if the death of Brandon Cunningham has a bearing on the Isabella Thornhill case?" the journalist said.

"No comment."

"Oh, come on, Chief Inspector. I have it on good authority that he committed suicide. Do you believe he was driven to it because of his financial shenanigans, or that it was because he was involved in the death of his sister-in-law?"

Livermore began to lose his patience. "As I've told you, Mr Dudley, I've no comment to make."

"Surely after the help I've provided, you can tell me something off the record," Dudley persevered.

"One thing I will say is I find it hard to believe that you, Mr Dudley, who were among the media pack labelling George Thornhill a wife killer not long ago, now seem to be suggesting someone else did the crime."

Dudley had a quick response. "I'm merely following my reporter's nose. You owe me, Chief Inspector, after the tip off I gave you about George Thornhill having an affair with his PA Raven Vickers. You never came back to me, but my hunch is you're looking at a sexual motive involving either Vickers or Cunningham. Just give me a steer."

Livermore, fully aware that the journalist would be writing something whether he made a comment or not, partly relented.

"OK, and strictly on an off-the-record basis, we're looking into the possibility a second person might have been involved in some way with the killing of Mrs Thornhill after being seen leaving the crime scene. I can't comment on any individuals, but you can no doubt let facts speak for themselves."

Dudley chuckled. "You mean facts about relationships? Like that between Isabella and Cunningham, and the relationship between her husband and his PA. If either Vickers or Cunningham was the person seen leaving by the back door of the crime scene it's probable they were the killer."

"You're entitled to express your opinion, Mr Dudley, but I have no official comment to make."

Dudley acknowledged: "Fair enough, Chief

Inspector. But if I can help in any way, let me know. I'm beginning to feel sorry for that poor sod George Thornhill rotting in jail for a crime he probably didn't commit."

Livermore's directive to dig deeper into everything relating to Brandon Cunningham brought a startling revelation when his team next assembled.

Helen Yates reported that the fraudulent businessman had three personal bank accounts, one of which showed several suspicious transactions. "A regular outgoing payment of particular interest to us was a monthly sum of £1,000 to an off-shore building society," she said. "I've checked this out and it was in Jersey in the name of Mullery - the maiden name of Isabella Thornhill."

"Well, well, well," mused Livermore." I wonder if these untaxed payments were for modelling work or for personal services rendered."

Dimbleby was quick to add: "Apparently both the Thornhills had guilty secrets. I always thought that their images were too good to be true."

It prompted his boss to speculate: "It could be that Isabella was having a sexual relationship with her brother-in-law and may even have been blackmailing him. If so, that would have given Cunningham a motive to murder her."

Tony Flood

CHAPTER THIRTY-ONE
Thursday, June 30th, 2022

Myra Thornhill was making her third trip to Thamesmead in South East London to visit her brother in Belmarsh prison and she hated the place.

On arrival at the prison's visitors' centre, Myra had her permit checked by staff and her personal belongings left in a locker before finally being allowed into the visitors' hall.

Myra, forcing her delicate features to give a warm smile, hid her feelings well as she again attempted to lift George out of his depression. She assured him that Livermore was following up on the sighting of someone leaving the crime scene.

"I wish I shared your optimism, Elfin," he told her. "I find it hard to believe that the police are likely to fully reopen the case after refusing to listen to what I told them and getting me banged up in here?"

His sister tried to convince herself as well as her dejected brother when she told him: "Livermore promised me he would check out that awful stalker as well as your brother-in-law. The fact that Brandon has committed suicide could mean he was the killer."

"It wouldn't surprise me if he was, Elfin. He was a slimy bastard. But he's not confessed to killing Isabella, has he? The police will no doubt come to the conclusion that he topped himself because of the financial mess he was in. And that may well be the reason."

Myra changed tack. "Have you been able to think of anyone else who might have done it?"

"No. I've racked my brains, but I don't know anyone who would actually be capable of attacking Isabella like that."

"Is there anything, no matter how small, that comes to mind, George? Was there anything different about Isabella that morning before you went to work?"

"Well, she was naturally delighted to receive her birthday cards and presents."

"Did she open the presents before you left?"

"Some of them. I think a couple were due to arrive later, like the one that Express Couriers bloke brought."

"Did she put any of the presents on?"

"Only the kimono I gave her."

Suddenly George remembered something. "One thing that does come to mind is that when I found her lying on the floor she was wearing a new necklace. I think it may have had her initials on it, but I can't be sure. She didn't have it on when I left for work and I don't recall seeing it among the presents she opened."

Myra's face lit up. "That could mean it was given to her in person - perhaps by the killer."

"It's a possibility," agreed her brother. "But the necklace could have been in the parcel the delivery man asked Isabella to sign for, couldn't it?"

Far from being discouraged, Myra became even more hopeful. "You've just mentioned the other person who was at the crime scene," she exclaimed. "Nobody's looked into the possibility that the delivery man could have attacked Isabella, have they?"

Myra could see that George did not share her excitement.

"You're clutching at straws, Elfin," he said, burying his head in his hands.

When he looked up she could see he was full of anguish.

"Sorry," George muttered. "I'm trying to hold things together, but I'm going crazy being banged up in here. And I keep getting the evil eye from this thug Mad Micky Moore - the bastard is getting a kick out of intimidating me."

"Has he hit you again, George?"

"No, but he spat at me when he walked past yesterday."

"Why don't you report him?"

"It's far better that I just keep out of his way, Elfin. But the worst thing about life in here is the feeling I have of complete emptiness."

Myra could tell from her experience of working with mental health patients that George was becoming increasingly depressed and might try to end it all if he got the chance.

Her thoughts were immediately confirmed by what he said next. "When my cellmate was sick last week and had to go into hospital for three days I seriously thought about taking advantage of being alone in my cell by making a noose and hanging myself. I can fully understand why Brandon ended it all."

Myra was horrified. "Don't ever think like that, George. You must never give up hope. Let me talk to Chief Inspector Livermore about the neckless - that could be a big breakthrough."

She so wanted to reach across and hug her brother, and it was tearing her apart that she could not comfort him.

One thought kept flashing through her mind: 'I must do something quickly!'

CHAPTER THIRTY-TWO
Thursday, June 30th, 2022

George found it hard to fall asleep that night - mainly due to the contradictory thoughts that were scrambling around inside his head as he tried in vain to get comfortable on a rock-hard pillow.

When sleep finally came it did not last long, and a terrible nightmare caused him to shriek with alarm.

He woke to find his cell-mate Fats Brown's large frame and bald head looming over him. "What the bloody hell's the matter with you?" demanded Fats. "You're making more noise than those nutters we're locked up with."

"Sorry," George apologised, becoming fully awake. "I've just had the most awful nightmare. I dreamed that I actually killed my wife. We had a row, grappled with a kitchen knife and she was stabbed, just like the police claimed."

His cell-mate remained silent as George shook his head in disbelief. "The bloody nightmare seemed so real. But I'd never do anything like that. I've occasionally had difficulty remembering things after a distraction, and the fact I'd taken several Sumatriptan for my migraine on the day Isabella was attacked might have caused me to become confused. But I'd remember doing something as terrible as stabbing my wife."

Fats' answer was not what George wanted to hear. "Perhaps the nightmare was real, mate. Maybe your brain's been trying to shut out the truth."

George was horrified. He told himself: 'There's no way that could happen - could it?'

CHAPTER THIRTY-THREE

Friday, July 1st, 2022

Livermore was called in to see Detective Chief Superintendent Frampton soon after arriving at Lewes HQ.

Frampton looked up from his paperwork and cut straight to the chase. "How are you coping without your right hand man Jeff Nottage?" he wanted to know.

Livermore wondered if his senior officer was showing genuine concern, or whether he might have some other motive so he chose his words carefully. "It obviously makes life more difficult, sir, but the team are covering very well. Of course, it would help if you are able to provide a temporary replacement."

"I was hoping to do so, Harvey. In fact, I had a detective inspector lined up, but the silly sod has got himself suspended."

Livermore was intrigued. "Who's that, sir?"

"It's DI Peter Cornfield, who's very highly regarded. I was arranging for him to join you on secondment from West Sussex, but I heard late yesterday that he's been accused of committing a sexual offence at a retirement party, and now faces a misconduct hearing. The point is it's now unlikely you'll get a replacement at this time."

Livermore nodded. "I understand, sir. Thanks for telling me. But I'm being given excellent support by DS Dimbleby and the rest of the team. DC Conteh is doing some sterling work and would make an excellent sergeant."

"Point taken," said Frampton, taking a note on the pad in front of him.

"So, although we're fully stretched, I think we can manage, sir."

"That's good," acknowledged Frampton. "Have you any further updates for me?"

The DCI explained about the possible implications of Brandon Cunningham's suicide note. "We're looking into that further, sir. But we're also continuing to investigate Raven Vickers and one or two others. I'll keep you posted."

+++++

Despite Myra's best efforts, she found it impossible to contact Livermore on Friday.

When she phoned Lewes police HQ she was told he was unavailable. The DCI was not in his usual cafe and another call also proved fruitless - Livermore was not in his office and his deputy, DI

Nottage, was off sick. She left a message, but wasn't hopeful of receiving a call back.

An impatient Myra soon thought of someone else who might be able to help, and phoned David Parsons. But his secretary said he was away and would not be back until after the weekend.

'I'll just have to wait,' she thought. But then another idea struck her. What about the journalist whose recent stories in the Argus had revealed that new evidence had come to light?

She managed to contact Dougie Dudley through the news desk and he agreed to see her. Within the hour they were having a drink together at a Costa Coffee in Brighton.

But her efforts to engage the help of the reporter were not proving as fruitful as she had hoped.

"So," Dougie was summarizing, "You reckon that Isabella could have been killed by a delivery man who she didn't know. With the best will in the world, I can't see that being the case. Your other theory is that someone Isabella did know turned up to give her a birthday present of a necklace and then stabbed her. That also sounds rather unlikely, doesn't it?"

Myra's heart sank. "When you say it like that, I suppose it does, Mr Dudley. But surely it's worth looking into. The police should at least find out if the delivery man has a criminal record, and who gave Isabella the necklace."

Although the reporter still seemed unconvinced, he wanted to know more about her theories. "Did your brother tell you what the necklace looked like?"

"He's not sure, but thinks Isabella's initials may have been engraved on it."

"Well, this might have been ordered online. But even if it came from a local jewellers it would be unrealistic for you and I to contact every one of them, asking if they sold someone a necklace bearing the initials IT. We haven't a clue whether it was purchased in Eastbourne, Brighton, Polegate, Hailsham or anywhere else in East Sussex. But the police would be able to do it. I'll get in touch with Detective Chief Inspector Livermore and suggest he has it checked out. He should also agree to look into your suggestion that the delivery man could have a criminal record - that is if he hasn't already done so."

Myra expressed her thanks, but reflected upon her brother saying she was clutching at straws. "What happens if you get fobbed off by the police like I did? Or DCI Livermore may be away for the weekend?"

Dudley, clearly not sharing her anxiety, replied: "If

that's the case I'll contact him on Monday."

Myra began to fear that the reporter might be simply indulging her, and fought to hold back tears. "You don't understand, Mr Dudley. My brother feels threatened by some thug in prison, and George is so depressed he's becoming suicidal. I'm terrified he'll find some way to take his own life if this drags on much longer."

"Leave it to me," said Dudley. "I've got a mobile number for someone in the police Press office - they'll get a message to Livermore."

Tony Flood

CHAPTER THIRTY-FOUR
Friday, July 1st, 2022

Livermore's curiosity was aroused by the message he received from Dudley. It simply said: "Sherlock Holmes had the answer to your case."

The busy copper was sufficiently intrigued to take the reporter's follow up phone call.

"OK, Dudley. You've got two minutes. What's all this about Sherlock Holmes?"

"I've been contacted by Myra Thornhill, Chief Inspector. She's come up with two more theories. At first I was prepared to dismiss them as far-fetched speculation by a desperate woman trying anything to get her brother out of jail. But the more I consider them, the more I realise that they would have been taken seriously by Arthur Conan Doyle's famous sleuth. They both fit in with what Holmes said."

"And what was that?"

"Once you eliminate the impossible, whatever remains, no matter how improbable, must be the truth."

Livermore was hooked. "Alright, tell me Miss Thornhill's theories."

After the journalist had relayed the assertions

concerning either the delivery man or a male admirer, Livermore grimaced. "I think your first inclination was correct, Mr Dudley. These are not just improbable scenarios more in keeping with a film script, but they carry no credence. Why on earth would the delivery man attack Mrs Thornhill? The only connection with him is that he could have delivered the necklace that she was wearing when she was killed."

The journalist's reply made Livermore reconsider, however. "What you say, Chief Inspector, is logical, but either of Myra Thornhill's theories could make sense if there was a sexual motive, couldn't they?"

Livermore pondered whether it was feasible for either the delivery man or a male admirer bringing a gift of a necklace could have been turned on after seeing Isabella in a revealing kimono. It resulted in him instructing his team to make checks into Donal McCarthy's background, and find out from local jewellers if one of them sold a necklace bearing the initials 'IT'.

CHAPTER THIRTY-FIVE

Monday, July 4th, 2022

Livermore's team could not find the answers as quickly as Myra Thornhill would have liked, but they had come up with comprehensive details about Donal McCarthy by the time the chief inspector called a meeting of Operation Butterfly on Monday.

Dimbleby reported: "McCarthy has never received a conviction, but three years ago he was charged with sexually assaulting a young woman in Brighton. He had a lucky escape because she refused to give evidence in court and the case was dropped."

"It seems we have a new suspect," mused Livermore, rubbing his chin.

Jones was able to provide more information. "That would seem to be the case, Guv," she agreed. "When I spoke to some of McCarthy's work colleagues, a couple of the women said he's a saucy sod who often cracks sexual jokes and makes suggestive remarks to them. One of them actually threatened to report him but he talked her out of it."

Livermore considered carefully what he had been told. "So Myra Thornhill's assertion about the delivery man being a suspect doesn't seem so far fetched now, does it?"

He told Jones: "Valerie. I'd like you and Chris to follow this up by going to see Mr McCarthy. Ask him if he went inside Isabella Thornhill's home when he made that delivery to her - did he ask for a glass of water or to use the toilet?"

+++++

At the next team meeting later in the day, Jones and Dimbleby reported that McCarthy insisted he had not gone inside the Thornhills' bungalow.

Jones explained: "McCarthy said he simply delivered the parcel to Mrs Thornhill, got her signature and left. He claims he was only there a few minutes."

Dimbleby licked the sharpness behind his front tooth before adding: "He was adamant. And when I asked him if he was disturbed by seeing Mrs Thornhill in her kimono, he simply said she looked 'fit'. He refused to reveal whether he was aroused."

Livermore felt that further evidence was required. "You need to follow up by talking to the neighbours again. Find out if any of them saw McCarthy make the delivery - if so, was it a quick drop off, or did he appear to go inside?"

Dimbleby raised his hand. "Do you mind if someone else goes with Valerie, Guv, because I've managed to get a dental appointment - this bridge that I had fitted is driving me crazy."

"OK, Valerie. Ask Mike or Brian to go with you - whichever of them is free."

While he was talking Conteh burst in. "Sorry to be late, Guv, but I've got some news about the purchase of the necklace," she announced after taking a quick breath.

"Fire away, then, Grace."

"We started contacting jewellers in and around Eastbourne and struck it lucky. The necklace was purchased from Goldsmiths & Myers. And because one of the initials on it was originally carved incorrectly, it could not be collected until the morning of the day Isabella was attacked."

"So who purchased it?" asked O'Sullivan. "Was it her late brother-in-law Brandon Cunningham?"

"No," Conteh declared, raising her voice dramatically. "It was the Thornhills' solicitor David Parsons."

Tony Flood

CHAPTER THIRTY-SIX

Monday, July 4th, 2022

Livermore was given a full briefing from Conteh about her visit to the jewellers.

She explained that the assistant who actually handed over the necklace to David Parsons was currently on holiday in Egypt so the jewellers could not confirm at this stage what time the solicitor had called for it.

"They should be able to tell by looking at their CCTV or finding the till transaction," Livermore pointed out.

"Unfortunately, they haven't kept the CCTV footage for that far back, Guv, and David Parsons had already paid for the necklace on a previous visit so that's when the till transaction was recorded."

"That's a pity. If, for example, Parsons picked it up late in the morning and then delivered it to Isabella Thornhill he would have been with her shortly before her death. When does this shop assistant return from Egypt?"

"Not for nine days," Conteh replied. "I've obtained her mobile number and rang it, but it's out of any network range."

Livermore tutted. "Well, we can't wait nine days to speak to Parsons. Let's have him in and see what he has to say for himself."

+++++

Prior to Parsons arriving at Eastbourne for interview, Livermore gave Fussy Frampton another update.

"Let me get this right, Harvey," said his senior officer, completely deadpan. "You now think the killer could be either the delivery man or the defendant's solicitor?"

Livermore cracked his knuckles but prevented himself saying what he really felt. Instead, he restricted himself to politely pointing out: "I think those are two of the possibilities that should be fully investigated, sir."

Frampton sought more clarification. "Are you now firmly convinced that we, together with the judge and jury, buggered things up first time round?"

Livermore kept his response brief. "Not completely convinced, but there are further indications that the conviction of George Thornhill was flawed."

"Well, Harvey, you'll have to come up with some hard facts before we can present a case against either of these latest suspects to the CPS."

CHAPTER THIRTY-SEVEN
Monday, July 4th, 2022

Livermore, who considered himself a good judge of detecting lies, wanted to study Parsons' reactions closely so he assigned himself to question the solicitor with the assistance of Conteh.

Parsons attended in casual wear - a smart blue blazer and beige chino trousers.

When Livermore told him what they had discovered he noted that the man looked uncomfortable before quickly regaining his composure.

"Yes, I did buy Isabella the necklace," Parsons admitted. "And I delivered it to her personally. I should have told you, but my visit was hours before the attack on her so I didn't think it was relevant."

Livermore scoffed. "How many hours before?"

"It was about mid-day, perhaps slightly later, but I was gone long before the delivery man saw her alive and well at 2.30pm."

The DCI studied the man's face to see if he could detect any signs that he was lying, but there were no changes in his speech pattern, blinking or other tell-tale indications.

"How long were you with Isabella?"

"Not long. I handed her the necklace; she put it on and gave me a kiss on the cheek. She told me about some of the other presents she'd received and then I departed."

Livermore nodded. "You didn't stay for a drink?"

"No. I explained that I'd just popped in and had to get back to the office."

"So why didn't you tell us about you being at the crime scene? You, of all people, must have known that was completely out of order."

Parsons now looked ill at ease and squirmed in his seat. "I thought it could be misconstrued that I, as the defendant's solicitor, was at the location where the crime was later committed. It might have been seen as a conflict of interest."

"And not done your reputation any good, either," the DCI chided.

Conteh had another concern. "Why did you buy Mrs Thornhill such an expensive present? Were you having a relationship with her?"

"Of course not. I'd been friends with her and George for years and was best man at their wedding. I didn't consider the necklace to be expensive compared to the sort of stuff I buy for myself. And I got a good discount on it."

This prompted Livermore to glance at Parsons'

watch and cuff links. The DCI then looked down and noted that the solicitor was wearing brogue shoes instead of his previous Dolce & Gabbana footwear.

Conteh made an observation. "I understand the initials had to be amended on the necklace."

"That's right. The jewellers put the initials 'LT' instead of 'IT' and had to change them. That's why it wasn't ready to collect earlier. Look, I agree I should have told you about me giving the necklace to Isabella, but my mistake didn't interfere with your investigation, did it?"

Livermore ignored the question. Instead, he said: "We'll be looking into this further and will probably need to talk to you again, Mr Parsons."

Tony Flood

CHAPTER THIRTY-EIGHT

Tuesday, July 5th, 2022

Livermore was delighted to hear that his hunch about delivery man Donal McCarthy had proved correct when Valerie Jones and Brian Hudson reported to the next meeting of Operation Butterfly on Tuesday morning.

Jones announced: "You were quite right about McCarthy, Guv. One of the Thornhills' neighbours did see him make the delivery to Isabella on her birthday, and actually remembers that he went inside."

"Yes," chipped in Hudson, "his van was parked there for some time."

Livermore felt a tingle of excitement. "This could be a significant development," he told his team. "McCarthy never mentioned he went inside the bungalow when he was interviewed originally or when giving evidence in court."

Dimbleby was quick to respond. "Like you said previously, Guv, he might have asked Isabella if he could use the loo or have a drink. But why did he keep quiet about it? - unless, of course, he was the one who attacked her."

"Exactly!" snapped Livermore. "Let's arrest him

and also search his home. I want all his shoes brought in so that forensics can see if any of them might have blood splatters from Isabella's wound. And while we're at it, let's apply for a warrant to search David Parsons' home as well."

O'Sullivan, perched on a desk at the back of the room, gave his view. "I can't see it being the solicitor, Guv. It would seem that Parsons is more of an arrogant plonker than a real suspect."

"Quite possibly, Mike. I couldn't spot any tell-tale signs that he was lying when Grace and I spoke to him. What about you Grace?"

"No, he was most convincing, wasn't he? When the shop assistant returns from holiday she may back up his story about him collecting the necklace in plenty of time to give it to Isabella well before she was attacked. Of course, it's so long ago, the shop assistant may not remember what time it was."

O'Sullivan seemed to take this as confirmation of his opinion. "Either way, it could leave Parsons in the clear"

"Has anyone else got anything to report?" Livermore asked, looking around the room.

Analyst Helen Yates shot up her hand. "I think Blodwen Knightly could still be in the frame, Guv," she said. "I've been looking through insulting messages on social media sites and come across several really nasty ones from a lady called Jeanette Randall. The wording of some of her insults seem very similar to those posted by Blodwen to Isabella, so I dug deeper and discovered that Jeanette Randall is, in fact, Blodwen writing under another name."

O'Sullivan responded: "It shows what a nasty cow she is, but why does it suggest to you that she might have attacked Isabella?"

Helen explained. "Blodwen's latest target is one of her neighbours, and the abuse on Facebook and Instagram has been going on for some months. It shows just how persistent, unforgiving and vindictive Blodwen can be. I think we might have under-estimated her. Perhaps she wasn't prepared to let things lie with Isabella - maybe she did decide to turn up and spoil her birthday."

Livermore had heard enough to convince him. "You've made a good case, Helen. I'd like Chris and Valerie to bring her in. Meanwhile, Mike, you can join me in questioning McCarthy."

O'Sullivan concurred. "If Chris is still giving odds, my money's on the little Irishman. He has a track record for sexual assault, gave false evidence on oath in court, and was inside Isabella's home with her at the time of the attack."

CHAPTER THIRTY-NINE
Tuesday, July 5th, 2022

When Livermore, accompanied by O'Sullivan, interviewed Donal McCarthy that afternoon he found the balding Irishman to be 'one of the biggest bundles of nerves I've ever seen'. Gone was the cockiness he had shown while giving his original evidence.

"So, Mr McCarthy, why did you go inside Isabella Thornhill's bungalow when you were only required to hand her a parcel?"

The delivery man's right eye twitched and his cigarette-stained hands shook as he replied: "I needed to pee. Mrs Thornhill was kind enough to let me use her loo."

"If it was as simple as that why didn't you reveal this when you gave evidence at her husband's trial?" Livermore demanded.

"I didn't think it was important."

"Don't give me that, McCarthy. You withheld vital information in court, and I want to know the reason why. I should warn you that we're searching your house and if we find any of your shoes or clothing contain blood splatters you'll be charged with murder."

"No!" pleaded his suspect. "I didn't touch her."

"Then tell us the truth," O'Sullivan cut in.

"Can I have a smoke? I need one."

Livermore ignored the question. "Just tell us what happened."

The eye twitched again before the little man finally answered. "I admit I fancied Mrs Thornhill like mad when I saw her wearing next to nothing. It gave me an erection and I needed to get rid of it which I did after asking to use her loo."

Livermore was not fully convinced. "Did you try your luck with her?"

"No. That's what I thought of doing at first, but I knew I'd land myself in a lot of trouble if I did."

O'Sullivan scoffed. "Remember, Mr McCarthy, we're searching your home so we're almost certain to find out if you're lying."

The Irishman looked alarmed and the shaking of his hands became more noticeable. "There's one other thing. You'll find a pair of Mrs Thornhill's panties in one of my draws."

Livermore's eyebrows raised, more in disgust than surprise. "And why is that?"

"I found them in her washing basket while I was in the bathroom and took them as a keepsake. She didn't know because I stuffed them in my pocket before I left."

The DCI glared at him and waited until McCarthy made eye contact. "That's one possible scenario. Another possibility is that Mrs Thornhill did see what you were up to and ran into the lounge to pick up a knife because she was scared. It ended up in you stabbing her."

"No" yelled their new suspect once more.

Livermore told him: "I will find out the truth. I promise you that."

Tony Flood

CHAPTER FORTY
Wednesday, July 6th, 2022

Dimbleby and Jones reported at the next meeting of Operation Butterfly that Blodwen Knightly had admitted posting the online abuse, and they informed her that she was being charged with criminal harassment.

"But the bitch insists she had ended her feud with Isabella long before she was killed," said Dimbleby.

"Do you believe her?" asked Livermore.

While Dimbleby considered the question, Valerie Jones provided an answer. "Blodwen is a very devious person, Guv, and it's hard to read her, especially as she's had so much Botox that some of her facial muscles have stiffened up."

Dimbleby joked: "We could hardly get a reaction from her - she didn't even raise an eyebrow."

Livermore showed his disapproval with a frown.

"Sorry, Guv," his veteran colleague apologised. "Being serious, I could detect Blodwen has intense feelings of anger and contempt for those she considers have wronged her. But her speciality is bad-mouthing people - not resorting to violence. On the other hand, she seems to be consumed with hatred and is therefore capable of anything. So I think the jury is still out on this one at the moment."

Livermore told his team that the searches of the homes of David Parsons and Donel McCarthy initially showed greatly differing results.

He said: "Forensics are still going through everything, but so far the search of Parsons' home, computer and laptop has revealed nothing out of the ordinary. McCarthy is a different matter, however. His living room contained an extensive collection of girlie magazines, and his laptop showed he has visited hundreds of porn sites."

O'Sullivan was quick to point out: "That's not really surprising, though, is it, Guv?"

"What is surprising," replied Livermore, "is the type of porn McCarthy prefers."

Dimbleby pipped up: "Is it illegal?"

"No," answered his boss, "not the stuff we've come across so far. We're still going through his favourite sites, but it seems the videos he prefers are those which 'spy' on so called innocent, unsuspecting women in states of undress. And, guess what? Most of them closely resemble Isabella Thornhill in both looks and what she was wearing when she was attacked."

Dimbleby, having had his tooth problem fixed, was able to give a long, low whistle of surprise. "No wonder McCarthy found her to be such a turn on."

There were no voices of dissent when PC Hudson added: "Everything points to McCarthy being the killer."

PART FOUR

CHAPTER FORTY-ONE
Thursday, July 7th, 2022

Myra Thornhill had reached a different conclusion to Livermore and his team. She marched past David Parsons' receptionist and burst into his office without knocking.

The solicitor looked up in alarm. "Myra. What's up?"

"You bloody well know what's up," she hissed at him. "How could you pretend to be helping George when all the time you've kept quiet about being with his wife on the day she was killed?"

"So you've found out," he said, apparently surprised. "I should have told you, of course. But what difference would it have made?"

This caused Myra to be even more angry. "Are you completely insensitive - or some sort of moron, David?"

"Calm down," he implored.

"I won't calm down. You've withheld important evidence, you bastard."

"Look, Myra, I've now informed the police I called on Isabella to give her a necklace, but that was hours before she was killed. It would not have prevented George being convicted. Now sit down and let's discuss this sensibly."

The irate woman took a seat. As she did so she saw that next to his desk were two suitcases.

"What's this? Are you doing a runner?"

For the first time she noticed that Parsons, dressed immaculately in a blue linen jacket and lightweight beige chinos, was starting to perspire.

"I'm simply going away for a few days," he said without conviction.

"If you don't start telling me the truth David, I'll shop you to the police."

"There's nothing to tell them, Myra."

"I think they'd be interested to learn you're all packed up and ready to leave just days after it's come to light it was you who gave Isabella the necklace."

"I've already explained that to the police," he insisted. "I simply gave it to her and left her alive and well. It was long before she was stabbed."

"Rubbish!" she snapped, glaring at him. "That's a pack of lies. I've been to the jewellers where you brought the necklace and they think you collected it much later. When the sales assistant who served you gets back from her holiday, I'm sure she'll confirm you didn't pick it up until a short time before Isabella was attacked."

Myra could tell Parsons was rattled and applied more pressure. "That's not the only mistake you've made, David. You've finally stopped wearing your favourite Dolce & Gabbana shoes, haven't you? Have you got rid of them? I bet you had them on when you killed Isabella and they were spattered in her blood. A forensics test can still show up the blood traces. You must know that as a solicitor, but never thought the police would check on you."

Parsons rose to his feet. "Bloody hell, Myra. Do you think you're some kind of Miss Marple? Or have you been talking to the police? Are you wearing a wire?"

His shorter adversary looked up to eyeball him. "Don't be stupid. I'm not as devious and cunning as you, David. But I don't have to be Miss Marple to know that when the police talk to that jeweller's assistant the game will be up for you. Now tell me the truth and I'll give you time to fly off somewhere before I report you."

The solicitor slumped back into his chair. "OK," he lamented. "I'll tell you what happened. I didn't pick up the necklace until after mid-day and got to Isabella's much later. She invited me in, and I was already in her lounge when the delivery man dropped off a package. The bloody man used her loo, but he wasn't aware I was there because Isabella closed the lounge door while she showed me one of the birthday messages she'd received."

He paused and wiped his brow.

"Go on!" Myra demanded.

"OK, OK. Isabella had not expected me to call and was only wearing a black kimono. She looked incredibly sexy, but was unaware of the effect this was having on me. She was delighted when I produced the necklace and, after putting it on, gave me a kiss on the cheek. As she did so her kimono fell open, exposing her breast."

He wiped his forehead again before continuing. "Isabella giggled. Perhaps it was in embarrassment, but I misread this reaction as being one of encouragement. I took hold of her breast and squeezed it. She tried to push me away, but I persisted."

Parsons paused and shook his head before revealing: "When Isabella said 'no', I lost my temper and told her not to be a 'prick tease'. It was the worst thing I could have said. Isabella shouted 'Don't call me that' and went ballistic. She grabbed hold of a knife she'd used to open parcels and thrust it towards me."

Myra questioned this. "You mean Isabella was scared and trying to warn you off?"

"It was far more than a warning. She was having a panic attack and about to stab me. I twisted the knife out of her grasp, and this made her stumble. The blade went into her and she fell on the floor, causing it to go in even deeper. I never meant any of that to happen - it was a complete accident."

Myra gasped. "What did you do then?"

"I was about to phone for an ambulance, but at that precise moment I heard George parking his car in the drive. So I fled through the back door."

"Where was your car? Why didn't anyone spot it?"

He gave a faint smile. "I'd stopped off to buy Isabella a card in the newsagents near her bungalow. I walked from there because it's usually difficult to park in her road. My only intention was to drop off the present. I hadn't planned to try my luck with her or attack her. It was just a terribly unfortunate sequence of events."

Myra did not show any sympathy. "But you should have helped her, shouldn't you?"

"I know," he admitted. "When I heard George arriving I panicked and did a runner. I knew he'd go to her aid."

"You're despicable!" Myra yelled. "And how could you let George take the blame?"

"I didn't know that would happen. When poor George tried to save his wife, he must have removed my prints and DNA by grabbing hold of the knife, taking Isabella's pulse and giving her mouth to mouth resuscitation."

Myra noticed Parsons' mood change abruptly as he turned to pick up his car keys off his desk. "Now, if you'll excuse me, I have a flight to catch and a new life to begin in the Far East."

She glared at him. "It's ironic, David, that you've only told me the truth after I lied to you."

"What do you mean?"

"I was lying when I said I couldn't be as devious and cunning as you. I've recorded your full confession on my mobile."

She removed her right hand from her coat pocket and opened it to reveal her iPhone. Glancing at the screen, she added triumphantly: "It's picking up our conversation very well."

Parsons sprung forward. "Give it to me, you stupid woman!" he yelled, trying to snatching the phone from her grasp.

A startled Myra was taken by surprise at the force of his attack. She staggered backwards, desperately trying to avoid falling to the floor, with her assailant on top of her. But another shock was in store as the door suddenly sprung open. In strode DCI Livermore. "Let her go, Mr Parsons," he ordered.

CHAPTER FORTY-TWO
Friday, July 8th, 2022

Livermore welcomed Myra Thornhill into his office and treated her to one of his rare broad smiles.

"Please take a seat, Ms Thornhill. Would you like a tea or coffee?"

"No thank you. Please call me Myra."

"Well, Myra, I don't know whether to give you a ticking off for putting yourself in danger or congratulate you on causing Parsons to make a full confession."

"I'll opt for the congratulations, thank you, Chief Inspector. But I must admit I was greatly relieved when you arrived to come to my rescue. I don't know how far David would have gone to destroy the recording I was making."

Livermore shook his head. "Fortunately the message you had left earlier on the office answer phone that you were going to confront Parsons reached me in time. I dropped everything and left immediately."

"You were my knight in shining armour!"

"Not quite. I did call for backup so the cavalry were close behind."

Myra nodded. "I didn't know for sure that my

message would get to you, but I thought I should try to keep you in the picture."

Livermore shook his head. "You shouldn't have taken matters into your own hands, Myra. We may not have been as quick off the mark as you, but were fully investigating the two leads you'd suggested. We'd already brought in McCarthy, and were about to arrest Parsons after finding out that he'd booked a one-way ticket to the Far East, even though we didn't have conclusive proof."

This prompted Myra to protest: "What about blood splatters on his shoes?"

"We haven't found his Dolce & Gabbana shoes so far. We did a search of his house and when they weren't there that made me suspicious. He wouldn't throw away something he'd spent so much money on unless there was a very good reason. But that wasn't hard evidence. And we're still waiting for the jewellery shop assistant to return from Egypt to confirm that Parsons didn't pick up the necklace until shortly before Isabella was killed. As you discovered yourself, that would mean he had to be at the crime scene around the time of the attack. How did you find which jewellery shop sold him the necklace?"

Now it was Myra's turn to smile. "I just got lucky. I vaguely remembered that David once boasted about getting good discounts from an Eastbourne jewellers so I started looking in Eastbourne. I thought he was a clever man, but he's been such a fool, hasn't he? In the end it was his ego that gave him away."

"Yes," confirmed Livermore. "His arrogance and conceit finally brought about his downfall. He even continued wearing his flashy shoes for months. He obviously never thought we'd find out that he'd been to see Isabella."

He noticed Myra was struggling to keep her composure. She eventually said: "You're right, Chief Inspector. David was the last person anyone would suspect of attacking her, and he counted on that. What I find so baffling is that he showed no remorse. Instead of trying to save Isabella or confess to what he'd done, David let George take the blame. That's unforgivable. It was all I could do to control my anger when I confronted him in his office. I had to call upon my experience as an actress with the local amateur dramatic society to help me."

"Your brother has a lot to thank you for, Myra. You've played a big part in revealing this miscarriage of justice."

"How long will it be before George is set free?"

"It'll probably take some time before his

conviction is squashed. But meanwhile he should be given bail very soon so he won't be in prison much longer."

"Try to get him out as quickly as possible, Chief Inspector. Isabella suffered a dagger to the heart physically, but George received a dagger to the heart emotionally. He deeply loved his wife even though he stupidly had an affair with his domineering, selfish PA Raven Vickers. I was able to speak to him on the phone this morning and he's so relieved that the truth has finally come out. But he said all he wants now is to be allowed to grieve for his wife properly."

CHAPTER FORTY-THREE
Friday, July 8th, 2022

Later that day Livermore phoned Nottage to bring his colleague up to date with events and find out how well his recovery was progressing.

"Congratulations, Guv. on finding the real killer. I'm afraid I got it hopelessly wrong in believing that the husband did it and getting him convicted."

"Don't be too hard on yourself, Jeff. The initial evidence pointed in that direction. Unfortunately, George Thornhill's frantic efforts to save his wife prevented forensics finding any clear indications of DNA from David Parsons. George even took her pulse on the same wrist that Parsons had grabbed in his tussle for the knife. So the only DNA our team discovered was that of the husband."

Nottage sighed. "Even so, I should have spread the net further and investigated other suspects more thoroughly."

Livermore gave a brief acknowledgement by simply saying: "Yes." Then added: "But the benefit of hindsight is a wonderful thing, and the family solicitor was the last person I suspected. It took the promptings of George's sister Myra to alert me to his involvement."

His colleague seemed to take comfort from this. "Thanks, Guv. Do you accept Parsons' version of what happened - that he didn't mean to hurt Isabella?"

"Yes, I do. As he said, he completely misread the signs when Isabella gave him a 'thank you' kiss for the necklace, and her breast became exposed. He thought she would welcome his advances, and when she didn't, he stupidly goaded her by calling her a 'prick tease'. What he didn't know was those were the same words used by a man who raped her years ago. Isabella had revealed to her friend Carlotta that a rapist had taunted her when she was a teenager. Apparently it had haunted her ever since."

"I didn't know," Nottage said. "What Parsons said must have acted as a trigger - a reminder of her past trauma."

"Exactly. I believe it caused her to have a flashback and panic attack when facing another sexual assault. No doubt Parsons' defence will be that Isabella over-reacted to his advances."

Nottage was quick to point out: "It was still assault, wasn't it? Furthermore, he did not try to save her, and he's shown no remorse. Parsons deserves everything that's coming to him."

Livermore concurred. "Ironically, he'll probably get the charge against him reduced to manslaughter by claiming he did not mean to cause such a serious injury. But it will count against him that he ran off, leaving his victim to die and someone else to take the blame. He could get between 10 to 15 years."

"And what about Raven Vickers? What do you reckon will happen to her, Guv? The vicious cow could have killed me."

"I'd like to think that the 'hit and run' will result in her getting a prison sentence. Donal McCarthy should also do time inside for giving false evidence. One thing's for sure - the little creep won't be making deliveries for Express Couriers any more. And hopefully Blodwen Knightly won't be posting abuse on the internet again."

Nottage expressed his appreciation. "By reopening this case you've put more than one wrong to right, Guv."

Livermore grinned as he contemplated his forthcoming meeting with Detective Chief Superintendent Frampton. 'I'm sure he'll be most grateful to me.' he thought.

'Perhaps he'll offer me early retirement on health grounds with a big fat pension'.

TONY FLOOD'S STORY

Tony Flood spent most of his working life as a journalist, initially on local and regional papers and then on nationals. He was also editor of Football Monthly, Controller of Information at Sky Television and enjoyed a spell with The People before retiring in 2010.

He recalls: "My work as a showbiz and leisure writer, critic and editor saw me take on a variety of challenges - learning to dance with Strictly Come Dancing star Erin Boag, becoming a stand-up comedian and playing football with the late George Best and Bobby Moore in charity matches.

"Now I spend much of my time writing books and theatre reviews as well as playing veterans football. I must be one of the oldest - and slowest - players in the country!"

Tony's first book was fantasy adventure SECRET POTION, which went to No. 1 in its Amazon category and has been recommended by other authors for Harry Potter fans of all ages. His celebrity book MY LIFE WITH THE STARS - SIZZLING SECRETS SPILLED! is full of anecdotes and revelations about showbiz and sports personalities, including Eric Morecambe, Elvis Presley, Kylie Minogue, George Best, Frank Sinatra, Joan Collins, Strictly Come Dancing stars, Muhammad Ali and Bobby Moore, with whom he worked.

The versatile Mr Flood then turned to writing in another genre with spicy crime thriller TRIPLE TEASE, endorsed by best-selling writer Peter James, actor Brian Capron and The Sun newspaper's Stuart Pink.

Following the success of TRIPLE TEASE, he wrote STITCH UP! - KILLER OR VICTIM? Once more compassionate copper DCI Harvey Livermore and his Major Crime Team are trying to put a killer behind bars in a new, gripping, fast-moving story. They are convinced that Denton

Kerscher is responsible for two murders even though he was acquitted of the first, but discover a string of other suspects.

Again, The Sun newspaper's Stuart Pink recommended Tony's thriller, saying "Stitch Up has a riveting plot and an electrifying double twist."

Tony has also co-written, with his wife Heather, LAUGHS AND TEARS GALORE – STORIES AND POEMS WITH TWISTS!

More details and special book offers are available on two websites as follows:
www.fantasyadventurebooks.com
www.celebritiesconfessions.com

Tony gives talks on the showbiz and sports stars featured in his celebrity book, as well as holding mini workshops and giving advice on how would-be authors can write a successful book. Any groups wishing to contact him can email tflood04@yahoo.co.uk

Tony and Heather are officials of Anderida Writers of Eastbourne. The link for the Anderida website is:
http://anderidawriterseastbourne.org.uk/news.html

Tony Flood

OTHER BOOKS BY TONY FLOOD

TRIPLE TEASE

STITCH UP! - KILLER OR VICTIM?

MY LIFE WITH THE STARS – SIZZLING
SECRETS SPILLED!

SECRET POTION

LAUGHS AND TEARS GALORE
- STORIES AND POEMS WITH TWISTS!

These books can be purchased on Amazon.co.uk
and other sites. They are also featured on websites
www.fantasyadventurebooks.com   and
www.celebritiesconfessions.com

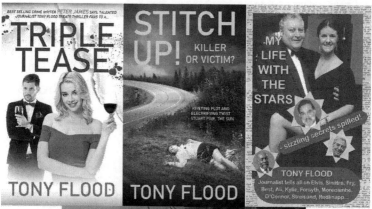

GIFT OF FREE BOOK

You can obtain a FREE e-version of one of
Tony's books by simply emailing
tflood04@yahoo.co.uk and stating which copy
you would like. You will then be emailed back with
the attachment of a complimentary e-version.

EXTRACT FROM TRIPLE TEASE

Here is the first explosive chapter from Tony Flood's crime thriller 'Triple Tease', the first in the series featuring compassionate cop DCI Harvey Livermore.

The expression 'drop dead gorgeous' was never more apt than in the case of Katrina Merton because some men would quite literally die for her.

She was a stunningly attractive 29-year-old blonde, with a dazzling smile, shapely legs and hour-glass figure - the nearest thing to a reborn Marilyn Monroe.

Katrina was fully aware of the effect she had on the opposite sex, and couldn't resist smiling when noticing a man watching her intently as she walked across the Westerfield College car park in Eastbourne on a dark, October evening.

Katrina was heading for a light blue Rover 45 in the right hand corner of the almost empty parking area.

The overweight man strode over just before she got to the Rover. "Eh, excuse me," he called. "My evening class has just finished and my car won't start. I was wondering if you could give me a lift to the railway station."

"Can't you just phone a breakdown service?"

"No I've got to catch a train to get to an appointment. You're my last hope - by the time I realised my car had packed up on me everyone else had gone."

"Yes, I'm usually one of the last to leave. I'm an art teacher and have to clear up before I go. OK. Jump in," she invited, clicking a fob to open the car doors and flashing him a sympathetic smile.

As they both slid into the Rover her knee-length skirt rode up quite high, revealing a glimpse of her stocking tops. She tugged on the hem but only succeeded in accentuating her full figure in a tight-fitting beige dress.

Suddenly his demeanour changed completely. "Are you a bloody tease?"

"What on earth are you talking about?" Katrina responded, alarmed.

"Forget about the lift, girlie. You and I are going to have sex."

"Are you out of your mind?"

"No, but you must be, parking in the corner of a deserted car park with nobody in sight." As he spoke, he pulled out a flick knife from his pocket and clicked the blade open. "Now, if you don't want me to cut that lovely face of yours, I suggest you do as I tell you."

His icy glare and the menace in his voice were compelling. "You're not the first woman I've 'had' in a car park. And sooner or later they do what I tell them. You can save yourself a lot of pain by unbuttoning your dress and showing me your tits - do it NOW!"

She met his stare and then started to carry out his instruction. The top two buttons were already undone and she slowly unfastened two more so that her dress fell open. Beneath was a low cut white bra with blue trim, which did little to hide a cleavage that would make Dolly Parton proud.

"I've been waiting for you," he said threateningly. "When you came out late last week I was going to 'have' you then, but someone else was still in the car park. Now you've left yourself a sitting target - a bad mistake, girlie."

He lowered the knife and started to fondle her by pushing one of his huge hands inside the bra and cupping her left breast. Her revulsion was heightened by his foul breath and a trickle of sweat dripping from his double chin.

"You shouldn't have taken so long to put the paints and brushes away," he mocked.

While the creep caressed her nipple she moved her right hand into an open panel on the driver's side and reached for an object inside it.

"Picture this," he goaded. "You taking off your pretty panties and handing them to me."

'You're out of luck,' she thought. Katrina replied: "No. You picture this - me shooting you dead."

She was holding a Smith & Wesson snub nose revolver in her right hand. "Now get your filthy hands off me, you creep. And drop that knife."

She noticed the look of shock on his face which slowly turned to one of defiance, but she held the gun firm and he finally did as she told him. The knife clattered to the floor.

"You say you've been waiting for me. Well, I've been waiting for you, too. One of those women you 'had' was my sister Suzie. It was in this car park three months ago and it left her traumatized. She's so terrified she still won't go out. That's because you not only sexually assaulted her, but afterwards you said you'd keep an eye out for her so that you could do it again. You bastard!"

"Oh, yeah," he hissed through a puffy pout which looked as if he'd placed his lips in a wasp's nest. "I remember her. She was a pretty little thing."

"You really are a nasty piece of work. The police haven't been able to do anything, but I knew if I set a trap for you in the same car park you'd probably try your luck again. Well, now your luck has run out."

"There's nothing you can do, girlie. There's no physical evidence and it will be just your word against mine. The police won't have a case."

"Who said anything about me involving the police? I'm not going to report you to the police. I'm going to shoot you."

He sniggered. "Oh, yeah, and leave blood all over your car?"

"It's not my car. It belongs to one of the students."

"Do you really expect me to believe such a load of nonsense?" he taunted, moving towards her menacingly. "Beside, you haven't got the bottle, so don't waste...."

He never finished the sentence. She pulled the trigger and a bullet to the heart killed him instantly.

Tony Flood

EXTRACT FROM STITCH UP! - KILLER OR VICTIM?

Here is the first dramatic chapter from Tony Flood's crime thriller 'Stitch Up! - Killer or Victim?', the second in the series featuring DCI Harvey Livermore.

Pippa Mercer was terrified as her assailant went completely berserk, waving his arms about wildly and striking her hard in the chest.

"That'll teach you a lesson, you bitch," the brute hissed. Pippa gasped in pain.

She knew she must get away and reach the sanctuary of her home across the road, but, hampered by her tight-fitting black mini-skirt, stumbled only a few steps before the man landed a second blow. "HELP!" she shouted. None came so she yelled at him: "Get away from me, you raving lunatic. I'd rather eat my own vomit than have sex with you."

That prompted him to go into another frenzy and he lashed out at her again. She fell to the ground, moaning in agony.

Despite covering her face with already bruised arms and hands, Pippa's lips became badly swollen and blood ran from a head wound. She made another frantic cry: "HELP, PLEASE HELP ME!" but still nobody came to her rescue.

Her attacker stood over her, gloating. "You pig!" she spluttered. Two kicks from the raging man's steel-capped boot crashed into the side of her head, bringing more blood pouring from a deep gash.

Pippa let out the screech of a dying soul before her torturous ordeal was finally over. She lay dead! The killer was still not satisfied. He pulled up her skirt and ripped off her light blue panties which he stuffed into his pocket before fleeing.

FALL GUY

Printed by Amazon Italia Logistica S.r.l.
Torrazza Piemonte (TO), Italy

41200066R00121